BORN INTO FLAMES

.

BORN INTO FLAMES

RECLAIMING HONOR™ BOOK 5

JUSTIN SLOAN

MICHAEL ANDERLE

DISRUPTIVE IMAGINATION®

BORN INTO FLAMES TEAM

JIT Beta Readers

Trista Collins
Alex Wilson
Kelly ODonnell
Johua Ahles
Keith Veret
Melissa OHanlon
Paul Westman
Micky Cocker
Erika Daly
Keith Verret
Thomas Ogden
Kimberly Boyer
Beck Young
Mayra Preble Figueroa
Ginger Sparkman

If we missed anyone, please let us know!

Editors

Diane Newton and Candy Clark

Thank you to the following Special Consultants

**Jeff Morris - US Army - Asst Professor Cyber-Warfare,
Nuclear Munitions (Active)
W.W.D.E**

CHAPTER ONE

The Eastern Coast, Former Canada

She was off her damned game.

Valerie dressed, almost failing to notice the pirate blimp passing in the distance as she glanced back at Robin stepping out of the river. Moonlight cast shadows across the younger woman's bare skin, shimmering in the droplets of water as they trickled down her breasts and thighs.

Had the blimp gone unnoticed, would Robin have not seen Valerie staring? Valerie bit her lip and turned away, embarrassed to be caught staring, and then froze as a different type of excitement took hold—there, on the horizon and traveling northeast, a dark shape moved slowly along the coastline. There was no doubt it was a blimp, and if it was up here, for her there was very little doubt that it was operated by pirates.

"It's the wrong way," Robin said, stepping up beside Valerie and picking up her clothes. She scrunched her nose and glanced back at the water.

"We don't have time to wash them, too," Valerie said, staring after the blimp, but very aware of the pale form of Robin beside her.

Robin pulled her shirt on with some difficulty as the fabric clung to her wet skin, so Valerie turned to her and helped. "But we want to be heading inland," her muffled voice said.

When the shirt moved down past Robin's face, the two stood staring into each other's eyes.

"You... looked like you needed help." Valerie realized her hands were still holding the shirt, and that the insides of her hands were touching warm, smooth skin.

"My pants, please?" Robin's expression was somewhere between annoyed and amused.

Valerie sighed, wondering what was coming over her, and turned to pick up the black pants. Kneeling, she turned to offer her friend the pants, only then realizing what an awkward position this was. She quickly stood and looked away. She thought it odd that a vampire should ever blush, but here she was, blushing like a ripe tomato about to burst.

"I'm just gonna be blunt here," Robin started.

"When's that not been the case?"

Robin laughed. "Someone takes your family away and forces you to become a vampire and assassin, you stop worrying about beating around the bush. And on the topic of bush..."

"My God, I was seriously just handing you your pants." Valerie said with a hand over her mouth. "I didn't mean to look."

"Yes, you did."

Hmmm. Maybe that was true. Shit, everything was so confusing. She pursed her lips and glanced over her shoulder at the young woman. "Is there a point to this, or can we get back to pursuing the damn pirates so we can tear their throats out?"

Robin shrugged. "I figure if there's something here that might distract you, we need to be clear about it."

"I'm not distracted."

Fuck, she *was* distracted, she realized as the words left her mouth.

She looked back at the blimp disappearing over the horizon

2

and frowned. When she turned back to Robin, the woman had turned away and was pulling her pants up, the contrast between the moonlight on her pale rear and the dark pants made Valerie stare again, and then shake her head to clear it.

"Okay, I'm totally distracted. I mean, but isn't that good? We've been walking and walking, and if I don't have something else to think about besides another day walking, or watching those fucking pebbles and the orange dirt, I'll rip out my own damn throat."

Robin pulled her pants up the rest of the way, zipped them, and then turned to Valerie with a smile. "Good. At least that's out there. Now, I'm freezing and wet, and not in a special way right now, because we just saw a pirate blimp, right? So, let's get on it."

Valerie stared, dumbfounded, as Robin started walking. She was so used to being the one that called the shots, or used to Sandra making plays but in a way that still made her feel in control, that this was a completely new experience. Jackson had been a leader, but there had always been a hint of something in his eyes that reminded her he was an unaltered human while she was a vampire.

Here was a young woman calling the shots and telling it like it is, and Valerie found herself enjoying it.

She caught up with Robin and decided to join her in focusing on the pirates.

"And Toro?" Valerie asked.

"We have no idea where it really is, except somewhere north of the lakes." Robin gestured to their left where, through the darkness, they could make out vast stretches of land that, even with their vampire eyesight, seemed to stretch on forever. "As you said when we took off, we wouldn't have a clue where to start."

"So, we take them down along the coast, get our answers, and then move inland." Valerie waited for the younger woman to nod in agreement, then added, "Great. I'm glad you're seeing the practical," she smiled. "Also known as my way."

Robin sighed. "I don't like it, but it makes sense."

Valerie nodded. She had an obligation to the people of Old Manhattan, and that didn't include wandering the areas of what was once Canada, searching randomly. She needed to stop the pirates from interrupting trade between Europe and Old Manhattan and had sworn to help Robin track down the slavers that had taken her parents. If they were lucky, her parents would be there waiting...

But Valerie was doing her best not to get Robin's hopes up.

Sandra rolled over in bed, the nausea of early pregnancy already making her want to punch Diego for making this her reality. Not that she'd trade it for a second—she wasn't some vampire set on dealing out justice. She was just a woman trying to survive in this crazy world, and in approximately eight months, a mom trying to keep a family safe in it.

That meant she had less than eight months to do everything in her power to ensure her world, or at least the world that could touch them, was as safe as possible.

Holding her own hair back over the toilet didn't exactly help her in that goal, but at the moment seemed a necessary evil. She dry heaved twice, then heard a pounding of footsteps behind her.

"Dear?" Diego said, kneeling beside her and holding back her hair. "Is this... normal?"

"Haven't known many pregnant women, huh?" The words came out with more of a bite than she had meant, but what the hell, she was pregnant. It was late at night, and she was in pain.

He could deal with a little grouchiness.

Diego thought a moment, "Honestly, none that I can remember," he replied.

She nodded, knowing that made sense. In times like these, people weren't eager to bring new life into the world. It happened, but even when people tried, it wasn't exactly easy anymore.

During talks with Diego at the small vineyard he had made for her, they had decided it likely had to do with the fallout of the collapse of civilization. Whatever had caused that had probably left lasting effects that meant childbirth either wasn't for everyone, or just made it harder to conceive.

They had laughed about it, and that night laughed some more while they joked about how they could go at it like rabbits and not have to worry about repercussions. And damn, could he bring it. She wasn't sure if that was the Were in him, or just *him*—not that it mattered, because him being a Were was part of who he was—but she couldn't believe the levels of ecstasy he'd brought her to.

And now, as another shudder of pain and nausea swept over her, she just wanted to slap him back out the door, to hit the wall and then perhaps roll down the hallway for even *considering* touching her.

Did every woman think these things during this time of the pregnancy?

The way he held her hair back with one hand and caressed her back with the other was certainly helping alleviate that feeling, though. She sighed, closed her eyes, and then pulled herself together.

Diego helped her up and squinted, apparently unsure what he should do here.

"I'm not gonna bite," she said, washing her hands, since they'd been on the bathroom floor and edge of the toilet. "That's your job."

He looked at her, wariness in his eyes. "Are you... coming back to bed?"

She turned off the water and dried her hands, then wrapped

her arms around him and gave him a loving kiss. With a smile, she took his hand and walked with him to the main room and the window that looked out over Old Manhattan.

The city was mostly dark but for the glow of moonlight and, in the direction of Capital Square, yellow and blue from neon lights. The view from their new home even showed Enforcer HQ, towering over them, its blue strip along the side lit up like a beacon of law.

They had been staying there before their journey with Valerie to Chicago, but since their return, they figured it was best to be out of the target area. Since dealing with the outside forces, the unruly of Old Manhattan had one main target, and that was Enforcer HQ. Not exactly the type of place you want to be when you're dealing with pregnancy and figuring out how to raise a family.

"Where do you think they are?" she asked, breaking the silence.

He wrapped his arms around her, creating the perfect picture of a soon-to-be family in the reflection of the window. "You worry about Valerie so much. Will it ever stop?"

"Yeah, yeah. I know, she's the most powerful woman around." Sandra leaned her head back so it rested against Diego's. He was on the shorter side, otherwise she would have been resting her head on his chest. Not that it mattered—he had certainly proven himself over and over, and shown that height had nothing to do with being a man or being able to protect your loved ones.

"The most powerful woman?" Diego laughed. "She's a day-walking vampire who doesn't need blood anymore to rejuvenate. That should scare you, not worry you."

"People with power tend to put themselves in dangerous positions." She paused, her voice whispering, "She's not invincible."

"But she has that assassin chika with her," Diego protested. "From what I saw, that girl could hold her own nearly as well as Valerie."

"You were watching?" Sandra bit her lip and rolled her eyes at herself. "Sorry, pregnancy brain. I promise, I'm not jealous or anything like that."

Diego rubbed her belly and kissed her cheek. "You'd never have any reason to be."

She pulled back, looking from him to their reflection. "Are we really as sappy as everyone says we are?"

"Tell me who said that," Diego replied. "I'll tear out their eyes so they don't ever have to watch us again."

"Or ears so they don't have to listen?" Sandra shook her head with a chuckle. "No, I don't think that's necessary. Let them talk if that's what they need to do to get over the fact that they don't have someone to love."

Diego squinted, looking her up and down. "Speaking of loving..."

"Are you serious, you just held my hair back, while I nearly puked my guts out."

"But nothing came up..."

"Yuck, man." She laughed, squeezed his hand, and then moved to the bathroom while he lay back in bed. She turned on the shower. As she undressed and steam fogged the mirror, she assessed her belly, wishing she could see more of a bump. She couldn't wait for it to stick way out, or for the days when she would be able to see the baby moving and kicking in there.

"Diego?" she said.

"Yeah?" he called from the other room.

She hesitated a moment before asking the question her fear drove her to ask. "If our baby is a Were, he won't like... try to claw his way out of me or something?"

His reply was quick. "Dear, I promise that's not something to worry about."

"But if it was, you wouldn't tell me anyway, would you?" She responded.

Silence. *That's what she thought.*

It didn't do any good to stand here thinking about it, though, so she slid back the shower door and stepped in. When she first felt the warm water cleanse her skin, all sickness and dreariness was washed away.

"Diego?" she called out.

"Yes, dear?"

"Don't go to sleep just yet," she said with a playful sing-song voice.

"Yes, dear!"

Royland crouched as he walked along a crudely-made roof of mostly two-by-fours and plywood. It seemed to be a lookout station. Too bad that hadn't worked out so well for the previous occupant, but now it made for a perfect viewpoint for Cammie and him.

The night was dark.

They had been observing the pirate outpost for several hours now, mostly to ensure it was actually pirates, but also to see if there were any vampires or Weres among them. So far, it seemed the answer was no.

This wasn't the first group of pirates they had come across, which kind of surprised him. When they set off from Old Manhattan, they had expected to come across one main pirate base where everything was being conducted.

Turns out, at least along the coast, a *lot* of pirates had gathered.

They weren't all Canadians, either, but groups from overseas —Spanish, Algerian, Laotian, and, most of all it seemed, Norse. Apparently, someone had been hard at work organizing the pirates around a cause.

Something, or *someone?*

Unfortunately for that someone, said cause conflicted with Old Manhattan's path toward becoming a conflict-free hub of the new world, or at least a new America. They couldn't allow interruptions in trade, and the idea of allowing a massing of criminals just north, on the same continent no less, was certainly unacceptable.

The first group they had come across was one of these ragtag groups, apparently on a scouting mission. Cammie didn't even bother hiding that time, she just walked right up, asked if they were part of the pirate group known to be stealing supplies via ship and airship interceptions.

"You bet your pretty little ass we are," a tall man said. He stared down at her over a crooked nose with eyes so dark they looked black.

"What, we steal your new panties and now you're looking to swap?" a fat guy amongst the group said, earning him a chuckle from the other three, all except the tall one.

She didn't even bother with a retort. Royland knew doing so wasn't her style, so he wasn't surprised in the least when she simply pulled out her kali fighting sticks and whacked the guy across the temple, hard enough to draw blood.

He stumbled back as the others froze in confusion, then she smiled, "As we were asking—"

But one of them charged her, doing his best to lower his center of gravity and pick her up. She was too fast for that and, with a twitch of her nose, was off to the side and had shaken the top parts of her kali sticks off to reveal the blades beneath. A downward thrust brought the blades into the area between the man's neck and shoulders, causing him to moan and then simply collapse at her feet, bleeding out.

The tall man turned his almost black eyes on Royland and stared, then held up both hands. "You with her?"

Royland nodded.

"You the same thing as her? 'Cause we have a hefty bonus

waiting for any that bring back the head of a Were, or any supernatural creature for that matter."

"Not interested," Royland said. "But I'm very glad you told me that."

"How's that?"

Royland smiled enough to show his vampire fangs, and then his eyes began to glow red. "Makes me feel better about my decision to kill you."

He lunged forward, Cammie taking the hint at his side and moving in for the fat one. The pirates couldn't have done anything about it even if they had seen it coming. With each action coming faster to him, he had taken down two before she took down her one. The tall man stumbled backward and fell, but Royland leaped for him just as Cammie was about to make her move.

She growled, and he smiled up at her, claws to the man's throat. "What, you wanted us each to get two? It was an odd number to start."

"That means you get the majority?"

"One of us has to." He smiled. "Tell you what, let's flip for him." He stepped back and, with one hand, lifted the guy by the waist of his pants to hurl him, spinning the man screaming into the air. "Call it." he told her.

"The fuck?" she replied. Then, seeing the man was about to land, shouted, "heads!"

The man landed with a thud, face down, and commenced with shouting obscenities.

"Wish I could say I was sorry," Royland said with a shrug to Cammie, then kicked the guy in the face to shut him up. "But this guy did insult me."

"How do you figure?"

"Well, he basically said he wanted to take your head, and maybe mine."

"And that's an insult to you?"

"You're my girl, after all."

"Hell no," Cammie said, and tossed one of her blades so that it landed in the pirate's side. She lifted her other one, preparing to strike.

"The hell?" Royland pulled the short sword free and tossed it back to Cammie. "I won the toss, fair an' square."

She caught it deftly, "And then you tried to claim ownership of me." She pointed the sword at him. "For which you're gonna have to pay." She sheathed the sword.

He stared at her for a moment, then shrugged his shoulders and waved a hand, "Ah, shit. Go on then."

The pirate started squirming at that comment, then shouting as Cammie pulled his head back by the hair, blade to his throat. Her voice was silky smooth, "What do you do with the supplies?"

"The hell are you talking about?" the pirate muttered, his eyes trying to see the blade.

"Whatever you intercept, or steal. Where does it go?" She asked the man.

He tried to stop this head from moving. "I'm a scout, not one of the raiders."

Royland nodded and stepped forward so that he could kneel in front of the pirate. "But you've seen where they go, haven't you? There's a home base of sorts?"

The pirate glared, then spat. "Go to hell."

"You fucking goat-cheese smelling dick," Cammie said, her knife digging into the man's throat.

Royland's hand shot out, catching her wrist and holding it from going farther. "Wait. Let's give this man a choice. He tells us and dies quickly, or," Royland allowed his fangs grow extra long and his eyes burn with red, "we allow me to slowly feed on him, until he's entirely too thin, and then kill him anyway."

The pirate gulped, but held strong. Or tried to, until Royland's fangs sunk into his wrist and the first blood started draining away.

"There's an outpost not far from here!" the man yelled, his eyes opened in fright as the man fed on him.

"We flew into one, just a ways south," Cammie offered.

"No, I'm talking north and a bit east. You can't miss it, but you've gotta be looking and know which direction you're headed."

"And maybe you're telling us wrong? Maybe you're leading us into a trap?"

He laughed, his bravado answering. "After what you just did to my boys? Damn right, it's a trap. But it's the trap you *asked* for. You go walking into a pirate outpost, even if it isn't the main base of ops, and I'll be seeing you both in hell in a couple of hours."

"Speaking of tearing and new ones," Royland said with a nod to Cammie, "let's get on with it."

Cammie's knife tore across the man's throat and Royland swept in to feed. It was a much-needed recharge after the cramped blimp ride and then the fighting.

The next two groups confirmed the direction, and Cammie even insisted they let one of the men live when he told them he had only just joined up with the pirates and had nowhere else to go.

"Head south to Old Manhattan," Cammie told him as she watched Royland feed on the man's dying companions, her chest beating at the sight. She licked her lips and turned her focus back on the man. "If you're truly looking to reform? They'll take you in."

He ran off, so scared he forgot to thank them for a second chance at life.

Now this blimp was arriving, and it became very clear that this *was* pirates, and that the flapping tents and crudely constructed buildings at the water's edge made up the pirate outpost.

Something bothered Royland as he watched the blimp touch down and then the men begin to unload. More ran out and helped, looking like ants scurrying about in the darkness. There was a sizable population here, it seemed, but the pirate who'd given them directions had said something about a main base of ops. Based on the way he spoke, that led Royland to think that the guy might have been former military, and that there was a much larger group of these pirates... and they were organized, at least to some degree.

"No use standing around staring," Cammie said, hands resting on her belt, cowboy hat tilted to one side.

"The sun will be up in a couple hours, I'd wager," Royland said.

"All the more reason to get in there and get rid of them ASAP."

He nodded and muttered, "Looks like I won't go hungry, at least."

"You know what I find hot as hell about you?" She laughed and gave him a shrug. "You're fucking hot, the way the blood drips down your chin when you feed, or how you almost caress the body as you drink, as if you're making love to it."

"What the hell are you talking about?" He frowned, thinking back to his feeding and wondering if that was remotely true. "Maybe you're putting something on me that isn't there."

She scoffed. "Just pay attention next time, you'll see. Don't get all self-conscious about it, I'm telling you it's hot as balls."

"Please," he shook his head in the night, "tell me you didn't just metaphorically compare my supposedly sexy drinking of blood to wrinkled skin that holds *reproductive spheres?*"

"Just a saying." She made a face and glanced at his crotch, then back up when he cleared his throat. "We can change it to something like 'hot as Royland drinking blood,' but it doesn't have the same ring to it. In your case, I'd say both apply."

He actually felt himself blush at that, then shook his head with a laugh. "You're an odd one, Cammie. And that's what I like about you."

"Yeah?" She waved him off as if the subject was played out. "So, get in there, or what?"

Knowing her way of talking, he had to be sure she meant 'get in there' like go down to the outpost and attack, not something else. He chuckled and said, "We kill pirates, find out where their main base is, then take shelter from the sun and tear each other to pieces, figuratively speaking, of course."

"I like your plan, big man." She was the first to step off, not even looking to see if he was following.

He loved that about her—confidence that he would follow. And he had no problem following someone like her. Especially when he knew where it led and what followed.

Although, he had to wonder if something was in the air with women this time of year? Or was it just Cammie?

He watched her as she glided away. *Nope, probably just Cammie.*

CHAPTER TWO

The Eastern Coast, Former Canada

Valerie walked along a small ridge, looking out toward the water in the distance, an endless spread of darkness, wondering how far they would have to go before reaching the point where the blimp had landed. She was certain it would be along the coast, so it was only a matter of time.

With sunrise coming soon, however, she knew time was a luxury best not wasted. Unlike her, with the ability to walk in the sunlight and not needing blood for energy, Robin was a young vampire. If they hadn't reached their destination and found shelter by sunrise, they could either set up camp, or cover the younger woman in the assassin clothes that protected her from the sun but made her look like a ninja.

Although Robin wouldn't say so, Valerie was fairly certain the woman didn't like wearing those clothes one bit. They had been what she was forced to wear by the vampires who made her, those same vampires that forced her to fight, although she had refused to kill innocents.

"How is it you avoided killing anyone, yet still had enough blood?" Valerie asked as Robin joined her and they continued on.

For a moment they walked in silence, their vampire sight helping them to see where they were going in the darkness.

When the first signs of red touched the sky over the water, Robin made a grunting sound, and then said, "It was Brad. He did it, pretended like I had so that I wouldn't get into trouble."

"And you two weren't a... thing?"

Robin scoffed. "I'm sure he would've liked that. But no."

It wasn't the first time Valerie had confirmed this, but she wanted to be sure. Robin couldn't give her full attention to the fight and search for her parents if even half of her heart was back there in Old Manhattan. That's where this Brad character now was, along with the rest of the surviving assassin vampires who had pledged their loyalty.

She knew that feeling all too well, and still laughed at the thoughts of when she'd gone after the blood hunters and sellers at the Bazaar. She had been so intent on killing them, while knowing Jackson was waiting for her, that she had even had thoughts of him in the middle of fights, flashing across her mind just long enough to be distracted.

It wasn't that she was worried about losing, or death. She wasn't worried at all, but she was concerned that distractions could lead to not accomplishing missions.

They paused for Robin to take a bite of jerky. She offered it to Valerie, who shook her head.

"We need to ensure we have enough for you, first," Valerie said.

Robin chewed, glancing over at her, then swallowed. "If we find them, my parents, what then?"

"I don't understand the question."

Robin pocketed the jerky and stayed there, hands in her pockets. "They'll be either dead, or part of a large slave community, I'd think. So..."

"We set them all free," Valerie said, frowning as she wondered why this wasn't obvious. "The people, vampires or not, responsible for making them slaves will face justice, and pay the price of such a crime with their lives."

"Do you always talk like that?"

Valerie blinked, taken aback. "I'm sorry, like what?"

"Justice this, justice that." Robin chuckled. "Can't you just say we'll tear their heads off and spit down their throats? We'll gouge out their eyes with our claws, disembowel them with a fucking spoon, or tear off their genitals with a rusty hoe?"

"Fuuu—uck." Valerie stared at her, wide eyed. "I could say all that, but then I'd have to sit in a corner, rocking myself to sleep in hopes that I could drive the images from my mind."

Robin eyed her. "Just seems more appropriate, is all."

"Do you ever wonder if the Black Plague vampires got to you more than you'd like to admit?" Valerie asked.

"Fuck you," Robin said, continuing the walk. "I have a vivid imagination. I'd like to see those vivid acts of horrible meanness inflicted upon the people who enslaved my parents. I can't think of anything more natural and pure."

Valerie caught up, bit her lip, and nodded. "You're right. Of course you are."

"So...?"

"You're going to make me say it?" Valerie rolled her eyes. "We'll snap their shins in half, then pull the bone from their flesh and use it to impale their hearts. Is that good?"

Robin thought about it for a moment, then smiled. "It sounds grosser when coming out of someone else's mouth."

"See, I told you!"

"But we're still going to do all those things, right?" Robin turned to her, eyes pleading.

"Damn, you look like a girl asking for a pony for Christmas," Valerie replied. "Of course. We'll do each of those things, even make a checklist and not rest until that checklist is filled with little, vampire scrawl check marks. Deal?"

"Deal."

They turned back, a smile on Valerie's lips, when she froze. "Do you see that?"

Robin stepped forward, narrowing her eyes. "It's either a giant butt or two blimps."

"I'd place money on the latter," Valerie replied, "and on one of them being the one we were following."

They crouch-ran along the hill, until they were at a closer point where it was very clear that what they had seen was the blimps, and that there was a small outpost just beyond them. Valerie ducked now, not wanting to be seen, and motioned for Robin to do the same.

Next, she shimmied forward, pulling herself along by her elbows and staying low to avoid being spotted in the moonlight by the pirate outpost below. She wanted to see what they were dealing with before charging in, guns blazing and sword swinging.

Orange dirt covered her arms and clothes now, but she didn't care. It was just one more layer of grime added to the yuck of walking for so long. Both were eager to move on and find their targets—the pirates disrupting Old Manhattan trade, in Valerie's case, and for Robin, those responsible for possibly enslaving her parents.

Valerie watched the movement in the night, a small outpost by the looks of it. Lights bobbed around like fireflies, but in reality, she knew they were men and women with lanterns.

The lights moved around the large blimp closer to them, showing something was being unloaded.

"These are the fuck-stick jerks who took our stuff," Valerie said.

"And the nose-bleeding dick sacks who will know where my parents are."

"The hell is a dick sack?"

Robin scrunched her nose, and shrugged. "Excuse me for not

knowing something I don't care about. We didn't exactly have class on the stuff."

Valerie shook her head. "A topic for another night. And... wow." She sat there, watching for a moment longer, then asked, "Did you swear this much when we first met?"

"It's an acquired taste," Robin said. "And it tastes better and better the closer we get to these pirates."

Valerie nodded, understanding that sentiment.

She was glad they had gone this way. Originally, they had meant to head northwest, having heard stories of piracy due north of the lakes where they had encountered the vampire, Gerard, and his followers. But there was something to be said about following the water, as the pirates at least started there and would provide a route from which to find the pirate haven referred to as Toro.

A ruffling sounded beside Valerie, and she looked over to see Robin, face-mask of her all-black assassin outfit pulled down over her face, though at night it wasn't needed for protection.

"You don't have to dress the part," she said.

Robin's eyes narrowed. "It makes me feel better about taking a life... pirate or no."

Valerie was about to stand up and lead the charge, when she put a hand out. "Maybe... we should proceed with caution?"

"You? Are you serious?"

"I mean, because we need to ensure someone's alive to tell us where to go from here." Valerie gestured toward the hills and vast darkness around them, only a hint of red from the rising sun kissing the tops of the hills in the distance. "We need someone to tell us."

Robin nodded, looking like she was about to say something, when—

BAM!

"The hell was that?" Valerie asked, moving up to a kneeling position to get a better look.

Again the sound came, and there was no questioning that it was gunshots. A small fire went off from a muzzle below, then more, and then someone screamed as a dark form moved among them.

Valerie and Robin turned to each other with wide eyes.

"We gotta stop them from killing everyone," Robin said, and then she led the charge down to the pirate camp.

CHAPTER THREE

Pirate Outpost

They hadn't meant for the fight to break out so fast, but Cammie blamed Royland. Her thought was that they get in there, keep a low profile as they see what they're dealing with, and then take them out.

She had, apparently, not communicated this so well. Communication over when and how to kill—her new relationship issue to figure out.

He had gone charging straight into the nearest group of them, not hearing, or maybe ignoring, Cammie's hisses of, "Wait! Not like that!"

It wasn't that she was worried for his life or anything like that, but this could cause panic, and that's not what they wanted. Half the pirates who had seen them were fleeing to the nearest blimp, the other half pulling strange looking pistols and rifles on them, a couple even with cutlasses.

Royland was, as ever, an impressive blur of manliness. The first pirate got a shot off, but then was hurtling through the air only to have his head explode as it collided with one of the structures, knocking the wall over.

The next pirate's throat was simply ripped out, and yet another's own cutlass lodged into his skull.

Three female pirates charged out of a side building, so Cammie turned to do her part against them. Since she wanted at least someone alive after this, she pulled out her kali sticks but left the wooden sheathes on, so they didn't become the short swords she was growing used to using.

As she charged, the first turned on her and fired—Cammie dodged, but then saw it wasn't a bullet or even a projectile, but a metal net. She rolled aside, just barely making it out of the way in time, only to be hit by a crossbow bolt in the thigh!

"Tarbaby-eating mother fuckers!" Cammie shouted, pulling the crossbow bolt from her leg. She would heal, but her anger was flaring to the point that it would soon be hard to stick to her ideal of keeping someone alive.

Tossing the bolt aside, she hobble-ran the rest of the way, her leg already feeling better by the time she reached them.

From there, it was thump after thump as she taught the net-shooter a lesson. Her stick smacked across the woman's blood-soaked forehead, and then the woman collapsed as another reached them—Cammie's enhanced strength and speed meant those blows flew fast and hard.

The second woman had an odd contraption on her arm that, when she punched, sent a series of darts out a split-second before the punch landed. It was large, made of a reddish metal, and was distracting enough to allow the woman to land the punch.

Cammie reacted by twisting one of her kali sticks around the offending arm, and turning so that her assailant ended up with her arm bent up behind her in an arm-bar. With an extended motion, Cammie pulled back her leg and brought her knee into the pirate's face. The force brought blood, spewing everywhere, and the pirate dropped to the ground.

Two men joined the fight now, and Cammie glanced over to see Royland with scattered bodies around him, the rest in full retreat for the blimp. To her annoyance, she saw that the blimp was starting to lift off. Pirates climbed ropes trailing over the side to get aboard.

Her muscles were slow to react when she tried to take a step toward him, and when a two-by-four hit her upside the head, she stumbled over, and fell.

What the hell was in those darts?

She knew that her Were abilities would fight it off soon, but when she turned at a shadow that fell over her, a boot connected with her face.

Damn, that hurt.

This time, she pushed through the poison, removing the darts, and then threw herself at the next attackers, no longer caring if she left any alive. At least, not in that moment as she tore through the pirate's shirt with her claws and drew blood.

These sons of bitches wanted to play rough? Bring poison into the mix? Well, then they deserved this. Shaking her head to clear it from the fog, she blocked a cutlass attack with one of her kali sticks.

With a growl and a gut check to pull on her energy, she caught the man with the sword by the legs, tackling him to the ground. Then she shimmied up his body, ignoring the crossbow bolt that hit her in the side, and then flicked off the wood cover of her stick to cut through the sides of his neck.

He screamed, but she shouted back, "It'll be easier this way!" Then, with a snarl as more poison darts hit her along with a punch to the side of her face, she grabbed ahold of his head and lurched to the side, twisting as she did so and using all of her Were strength to pull.

The head resisted, then, with a pop, came free.

Another punch hit her, and she fell, head clutched in her hands.

"The fuck's wrong with you?" one of the pirates said, pointing what looked like a shotgun into her face.

In a blur, the pirate was gone. Two more fell dead nearby, and then Royland was at her side a moment later, helping her to stand.

"I'm fine!" she said. "Stop the blimp!"

He nodded at the headless man and said, "They're right, that was nasty."

She smiled and then pointed at the blimp.

"Yeah, yeah," he rolled his eyes as he turned from her, "stop the blimp."

She took a wobbling step, nearly tumbled over, and then pushed through the pain and exhaustion that came with the poison, wishing her healing powers would kick in faster.

At least Royland was still in good condition, charging forward faster than the pirates could see. He took down another two, tossing them behind so that they were still shaking in their final moments of death as Cammie passed them in her attempt to catch up.

The poison was nearly gone when she saw Royland reach the first rope, but then she sniffed and cursed—more pirates behind her.

She spun and caught the first punch, this time pushing up the gloved hand before the darts could hit her. Another came at her and she broke the offending arm, then used it to punch the pirates companion. Darts flew out and, a moment later, the second pirate was writhing in pain, froth coming out of his mouth.

"Damn," Cammie said. "I'm sure glad I'm not you."

Her smile faded as a clunking sound came from nearby, then metal ropes of a net fell over her and she was pulled to the ground as it cinched around her feet. More blows came, and then one of the pirates turned and shot something that sent a rope to the second, still grounded ship, and she watched in horror as he attached it to her feet.

"Oh no you don't," she said as she pushed against the net, but the pirate simply smiled and pressed a button on the device. A second later, she was whisked away, the rope retracting, pulled along the ground in a way that seemed to be purposely slamming her into each rock. It was only then that she realized the second ship was starting to take off now, too, and as it did, she was lifted off the ground and pulled up right alongside it.

She twisted as best she could, weighing her options as the ground disappeared beneath her. Holy crap, she realized as she saw the other blimp start to go down.

Not only would she never live this down—her getting captured while he succeeded—but she had now been captured a second time. If she didn't break out, and soon, she would have to be rescued.

Dammit, she hated having to be rescued.

And to make it worse, her cowboy hat had fallen off somewhere during the fighting. Her swords were still on her, though, so she pulled one free and tried taking it to the metal ropes. Nope, that wasn't doing any good.

"Royland!" she shouted, and a moment later saw him appear on the blimp beside them. He saw what was happening, apparently, and ran to the edge of his blimp as a rope went by, then leaped...

...and missed.

She tried to turn to see what happened, but the ropes had her in a position that made moving anymore impossible. Shouting, she pushed, shoving and squirming in spite of the metal tearing into her flesh.

It wasn't that she was so terrified or feeling helpless, it was that she wanted to make enough noise to not hear a thud or screams of pain. Not from him.

"FUCCCKKK!" she screamed, and then paused, interested in another set of gunshots sounding in the distance.

What the hell were they shooting at? She breathed, forcing herself to be calm, and watched as two figures in the pink glow of

JUSTIN SLOAN & MICHAEL ANDERLE

sunrise cut through pirates. Swords flashed as the sunlight came over the hills, and she saw that one was all in black.

Like the assassins that had come after Valerie. She couldn't make out the other, but was pretty sure that this wasn't a good sign.

The sunlight on the swords meant something even worse, though. If Royland was hurt down there, unable to defend himself and pull himself to shelter, the sun would soon reach him, and take him from this world.

Finally, for probably the first time she could remember, a tear welled up in her left eye. When she had wiped it away, she gritted her teeth and said, "Wo-man up, girl," and renewed her struggles to break free.

This wasn't about to happen. She wasn't going to let some pirate pricks dictate how and when Royland left her, and she certainly wasn't going to be tied up in the air while he screamed in agony.

She would break free and save his ass, or die trying.

The moment the shooting had started, Valerie and Robin had given up all hope of staying concealed. Instead, they had charged the pirates, though staying at a run only slightly faster than normal humans, so that Robin wouldn't lose her strength.

Screams sounded and it was clear someone was in trouble, so the last twenty feet Valerie had sped through like nothing, pulling her sword free and cutting through the first group of pirates before they knew what was coming.

Surprisingly, the majority of them were scrambling onto the ships, though some had just appeared in a nearby building and were firing pistols and one rifle at her.

Instead of bothering to duck and hide, she ran at them, careful to avoid the bullets and the unnecessary pain they brought with them. Even with the Dark Messiah's blood flowing through her and giving her greater powers than she had known possible, she still hated pain.

That's why, when one of the bullets hit her, she pushed out with fear to such an extent that she heard bowels letting loose and the accompanied swearing before she was on them, sword swinging and wishing she didn't have such a strong sense of smell.

Others were running now, and she looked back to see the sun touching Robin, where the younger woman took on three pirates by herself.

If only one of them cut through Robin's clothes and exposed her to the sunlight, it would be a very bad day for everyone involved.

Luckily for them, Robin was a trained assassin and damn skilled with a sword, and her clothing was more like body armor in the places that mattered.

She turned back to the blimps, confident that Robin could handle herself, and watched as one rose while the other was in its descent. What the hell was going on here? She charged forward, then noticed a group of pirates sliding down from ropes attached to the descending blimp, converging on a form on the ground.

It appeared to be a man, struggling to stand, but as he got to his knees, one of the pirates shot him and he fell back.

A scent carried in the wind and she froze. Not only was it a vampire, but she had smelled this vampire before. It wasn't strong enough that she knew who it was, but there was no question in her mind that this assault had to be stopped.

Even if she hadn't known him, he was being attacked by pirates. So, maybe he wasn't so bad.

She reached to the pistol at her hip as she stepped forward, sword at the ready, and said, "Hey, spineless shit-stains, you want some?"

The closer pirates turned to her with smiles on their faces

that quickly vanished as they saw her eyes glowing red. She smiled to reveal her fangs, long and sharp, and then charged.

Her pistol tore into them, her sword finishing them off.

They didn't stand a chance and, as she brought her sword up and through the last of them, she stood in a circle of decapitated bodies.

Her eyes fell across them all, wishing she had at least had the chance to interrogate them, and then she saw their victim.

"Royland?" she asked in disbelief.

He had a hole in his cheek, limbs apparently broken, and seemed barely able to turn his head, but he saw her and mumbled something.

"What is it?" she knelt next to him and took a vial of blood from her jacket, then forced it down his throat while holding the hole in his cheek shut, so that it wouldn't spill.

When he had his fill, his finger twitched, then moved again, and finally he was able to lift it to point to the blimp that was still rising.

"Something's on the blimp?"

His mouth moved and there was no question what he was trying to say.

"Cammie is on that blimp," Valerie said in realization. "And judging by your condition, I'm guessing she's not much better off."

He didn't deny it.

A second later Robin appeared at her side, one sword in each hand. "What's the play?"

Valerie furrowed her brow, watching as the other blimp began to rise back up now, too.

"Move, fast," she said, and bent down to sling Royland over her shoulders.

"Where to?" Robin asked.

"We're catching that blimp."

Robin stared at her with wide eyes, but then said, "Got it," and took off for one of several ropes that were still close to the ground.

Valerie wasn't far behind, carrying Royland like a rag doll, doing her best to ignore the grunts of pain with each step.

"You don't want pain, stay out of the way," she said. "Or better yet, next time stay in Old Manhattan until you've talked your foolish plan out with me after I return."

He grunted a response, or maybe it was just more pain causing the sound, but she didn't care. She was too busy hoisting him over her back and wrapping his arms around her.

"Hold on," she said. "If you want any chance of making this and rescuing Cammie, hold on with everything you've got left."

Then she grabbed the last rope that was near the ground, and a moment later she was climbing, hand-over-hand up the rope with him clinging to her. A cursory glance showed her that Robin was shimmying up a rope nearby, almost to the top.

"This is insane," Valerie said as she saw the camp fading away below and started the arduous process of climbing that rope while holding onto Royland. "But damn fun."

CHAPTER FOUR

Old Manhattan

The sun had only just risen, but already Sandra was up, so she figured she might as well check on the new recruits. She hadn't been able to go back to sleep since her early-morning fun with Diego.

Valerie had once had a vision for the former police when combined with the new Weres and vampires—that they could be more of a military, set up to not only ensure peace within the walls but to patrol surrounding areas and even be ready to go on the offensive if need be.

This was Sandra's goal now, working with Colonel Donnoly and the others to set up this military. Upon returning from Chicago, they came to an agreement that it was necessary. The police would serve as the internal peace keepers, not losing their title, but set up in a much more formal role within a broader military organization.

Some of them, however, would join teams of Weres to make up the crux of the external military. A large portion of these groups would come from the recent recruits, Weres who had joined them from groups such as those from the Golden City.

They would each have one of the assassin vampires, at a minimum, who had brought their gear for surviving in the daylight with them. Even with the gear, they would serve as night watches, only expected to act in the day during emergencies.

Sandra's pod came to a stop at the edge of the east side of Central Park, renamed for the old days because the last month had been spent cleaning up this portion of it. They had established it as training grounds for their new military, in part because they needed the land, and in part because it allowed the citizens of Old Manhattan a view of what was happening. They might be inspired to join, or at least feel that much more secure knowing a real military was taking charge and working to protect them.

While she wanted to relax and run her café, the part of her that had lived with Valerie so long couldn't just turn away from all of this. She had to be a part of ensuring the city was safe. Maybe it was trust issues, she wasn't sure, but she knew that if she didn't help, she wouldn't ever feel certain the necessary was being done.

The abandoned ruins at the edge of the park worked for training in urban environments, and that's where Sandra turned her attention this morning.

"Can't believe these assholes still got us doing this," she overheard one of the new vampires saying, going silent when he noticed her. He nodded and returned to sparring practice with another vampire, both from the Black Plague assassin academy.

Their training was the most important, not to actually teach them fighting skills, but to ensure they stayed in line, to form the bonds of warriors.

She understood all of this from her years in France, under the Duke, and Valerie's brother. There had been no shortage of military training, both in combat and strategy. Valerie had been part of it, too, but there was something Sandra noticed about the more powerful vampires and Weres in situations like this—they didn't pay attention as closely as the weaker ones did. The more powerful ones, she had come to realize, didn't have as much to worry about, or so they always seemed to think when being taught something. This was especially true when the teacher was less powerful, and even more so when the teacher was an unaltered human. A normal, boring human. Like her.

That's why she didn't teach what she learned while under the Duke, or if she did, it was behind closed doors, talking strategy with Colonel Donnoly and the others. They could take it or leave it, but they had begun to listen more and more to the girl with the café. The girl who had been best friends with the most powerful vampire in Old Manhattan, while Valerie was here.

Now, the most powerful vampire—Diego surmised at night lying together with Sandra and discussing the future of the city— was likely this new guy, Brad. And they discussed the city's future often, because now Sandra had been certain she was pregnant for over a month and, while that still wasn't much, every day made it more of a reality. They were bringing another life into this world, and needed to ensure it was a better world before that happened.

Sandra stopped to watch Brad leading his squad, a mash up of former assassins and older vampires. Brad commanded the vampires to defend against a throat grab, then turned to practicing sword technique. They focused on blocking first, especially the neck, as a vampire being decapitated was an easy way to end their lives and leave them without a way to heal.

One of the vampires hit another too hard, and the second responded by charging him, but was felled by a quick blow across the forehead from the one who had been attacked.

The training wasn't over, but Sandra felt slightly queasy again and decided she needed something in her belly. Preferably a warm, chocolate pastry. It hadn't been too hard to pull together some old ovens out of the ruins and, with Diego's help, they'd soon been able to organize the kitchen in her café to be able to make croissants, her favorite from the days before. She didn't really remember those days, not exactly, but she remembered the scent of warm bread, the flaky crust as she bit into it, and the wrinkles around her dad's loving eyes as he smiled and wiped chocolate from her face.

Losing them had been the single worst day of her life, so bad that it had made the horrors of being a slave to vampires almost meaningless. She was numb, didn't want to live, and certainly didn't give a damn what they did to her.

That was, until she was assigned to Valerie and everything had changed. Valerie had been loving, treated her like a human, or like a vampire, even. She had looked her in the eyes when talking, and never once struck her.

When they had left their old lives behind and Valerie had declared the old ways over as well, they were officially equals again, but nothing changed—they had been equals all along, both constrained by the chains that held them to the ways of the so-called Blessed. The Duke was scum, a piece of dog shit stuck on a shoe. And now the vampire Michael had gone to wipe that shit away.

Sandra asked Peter, the driver of her pod, a nice man with gray hair hanging low over his shoulders, to take her to the cafe. She leaned back, thinking about Michael, wishing she could have met him. She would have loved to shake the hand of the vampire who was going to kill the Duke. Even better if she could go with him and watch as he ripped the lower vampire's throat out. Regardless, she'd toast his death. Or she would once this baby came out and she could have alcohol again.

Damn, she'd kill for a nice glass of anything, right about now.

The pod came to a stop in the alley beside the café, and she thanked Peter. He insisted on helping her out, only convincing her when he said that Diego would tear off his legs and beat him with them if he didn't, and Diego caught wind of it.

She took Peter's hand and stepped out of the pod, glad to have him there as she felt herself nearly fall.

"Shut up," she said at the sparkle in his eye. "And thank you."

He laughed. "You going to be long? I only ask because I haven't slept, and—"

"Why the hell haven't you slept?" She was about to leave it be, when she saw him blush. "Oh, come on. Don't tell me the details, but… really?"

"You don't want to hear the details?"

"I know, I just said that." She shook her head, laughing. "Not that I've been any better, but what is it about a torn apart world that makes everyone get all screwy?"

"Pun intended?" He laughed. "Maybe it's the fact that we've seen so much death and destruction, we know the next day could be our last."

"Yeah, maybe that. Maybe we crave extra comfort to get us through these bleak times."

"Or maybe we just like to fuck."

She hit him, playfully. "Watch your mouth in front of a lady."

He tipped his non-existent hat and said, "My apologies. I mean, sorry for not knowing you were such a prude."

"Hey, I like to get down as much as the next gal. I'm just saying there's going to be a baby here soon, and if you talk like that around him, I'll slap your face off."

With a laugh he said, "I don't doubt you would."

"See ya, Peter." She gave him a mock salute, something she had started doing recently, though she didn't really know why, and laughed at herself.

What was she doing up so early? She glanced out at Capital Square and saw the usual homeless people on the far side, mostly trying to sleep but a couple eating some scraps they had found. At least she wasn't the only one up in the city, though she found it humorous that it was pretty much just the homeless, the new army, and her.

She fumbled with her key and got the back door open, mouth watering at the thought of those chocolate croissants. The craving was so real, she could swear the scent of the fresh dough was already in the air.

At first her keys didn't turn, so she had to jiggle them and then shove the door with her shoulder, and then she froze. There was no doubt about the croissants now—a tray of freshly rolled dough and chocolate sat on the counter, the oven emitting a warm glow.

"Diego?" she asked. "Where'd you learn to make croissants?"

A clatter came from the other room. She took a step back as the silhouette of a man nearly twice Diego's size appeared from behind the curtain. Her hand reached for any weapon she could find, and landed on the tray of croissants.

"Not those!" a rough voice said, "Hit me with whatever you need to, but oh my God, please let me have a croissant."

She froze, tray in the air, careful not to spill its contents, and then smiled as recognition hit her. The man had just poked his head around the curtain—he was tall, muscular, and had black hair closely shaven on the sides and short on top.

"Sergeant Garcia, what…?"

"What am I doing here?" He entered now, hands up to show he meant no harm. "People said this was where I could find you. They also said your croissants were to die for, so I thought I'd take my chance."

"You nearly did die for them," she said with a chuckle, lowering the tray back to the counter.

"Death by cooking tray." He laughed, too. "It wouldn't be worth it if I didn't even get to taste them, though."

"Wait, so someone tells you I work here, then you break in and decide to help yourself?" She waited, hands on her hips. "W.T.F., Sergeant?"

"Did I mention the part about croissants?"

She relaxed slightly at that. After all, anyone who worked with Terry Henry Walton was okay by her.

"Wait, how do you even know what croissants are?"

35

He smiled and said, "I didn't, but found your recipe and figured that, if anything was to die for, I better try it out."

She glanced back at the tray of croissants. "Not perfect, but not bad for someone who had no idea what they're doing."

"I know my way around a kitchen."

"But you've never tried croissants?"

He shook his head.

"Then, good sir, I'm about to blow your mind." She adjusted the temperature in the oven—because it wasn't in perfect condition and she was the only one who knew it well—waited a moment, then slid the tray of uncooked croissants in.

When she turned back to him, Garcia was leaning against the counter, looking at the bottles of wine and counters of cheese.

"You New Yorkers sure have it different," he said.

"If I remember correctly," she replied, "you all served steaks the last night we were in Chicago."

"I said different, not necessarily better."

"Wait until you try the croissants, then we'll see." She opened a pitcher of water and poured them each a drink. After handing him his glass, she took a long swig of her own and said, "I hope this isn't a social call. You know I'm seeing Diego and have a bun in the oven."

"Croissants and a bun?" He winked, then glanced down at her belly. "What a magical life you live."

"Your point for being here?" she asked, sternly.

"Ah, yes." He sat down this time, and she followed, sitting across from him. He cocked his head, then said, "Where's Valerie?"

"She went north to deal with that pest problem she kept talking about."

"That puts a damper on things, but assuming she'll be back eventually… TH has a proposition."

"He couldn't have made this proposition when we were out there?"

"Sure, he could have." Garcia leaned forward, smiling. "But I liked the idea of traveling out here to see you again, and since it fits into the plan…"

"You're losing me here."

"Okay, TH has been working for a while to secure America. He had this area down for a while, but it's hard to keep all of the continent secure, you know what I mean?"

"It's hard to keep our backyard secure, so yes."

"So, he gets to thinking—what if we partnered up?" Garcia smiled now, revealing how much he liked this plan. "We send someone strong, who knows what they're doing, to help train your fighters. Then we form a coalition of sorts, working together to keep it all secure."

Sandra glanced around, wishing she hadn't finished her water but not wanting to get up to fetch more. Not right now.

"You realize most of our fighters are Weres and vampires, right? I mean, they know how to fight."

"They know how to brawl, or how to kill," he admitted. "What they don't know is cohesion, how to operate as a unit. With discipline and integrity."

It was true. She was doing her part, as were Donnoly and the police force, but none of them were military. None of them really knew anything about external defense, aside from the intense butt-kicking they'd given the bad guys over the last couple of months.

"You're going to stay here and help us train?" she asked.

"Fucking A."

"And there's no misguided idea that TH will be in charge of us, calling the shots or something?"

"As I said, this is more of a collaboration, a partnership."

She smiled and stuck out her hand. "I think we need to celebrate with some amazing chocolate croissants."

"I think you're right," he said as she shook it.

She stood and went to the oven, then laughed. "Right, of course we still have a bit to wait. Damn."

"I ain't in a rush," he said. "Maybe some of that wine?"

"This early in the morning?" She shrugged. "That's how it's done."

She stood and poured him a glass, then sliced some of her favorite cheese. A glass of wine actually sounded perfect, but not with the baby growing inside of her.

"Everything settled down out west?" she asked.

"TH keeps everyone in check, as long as there're no super powerful vampires or CEOs running around. We still have to properly thank you all for taking care of that, by the way."

"And this space mission that TH mentioned?"

Garcia's smile faded momentarily, but then he shrugged. "Far as I know, there's a bigger battle going on. One that, if the vampires and their kind can't win, none of what we're doing here to survive will matter."

"Well, shit." She swallowed, considered that, then scrunched her eyes. When she looked up at him, her voice came out lower. "It's true then? I mean, there're other beings out there? Aliens?"

He nodded. "That's what TH says, and honestly, I wouldn't doubt him on much. Shit, he could tell me my balls were diamonds and I'd probably try to sell 'em for some extra coin."

She just stared at him, unblinking.

"Damn, lady, it's a joke." He shifted uncomfortably. "You New Yorkers aren't into jokes?"

"Sorry, just… it's a lot to process. And no, I don't mean your balls, which I'd prefer to not hear jokes about. Why is it soldiers are always making jokes about down there?"

"Imagine having a huge bulge in your pants, and it never goes away," he said with a grin. "It's going to be always on your mind, right? How can it not be?"

"There you go again." She shook her head, at least allowing a small laugh this time.

"Okay, New Yorkers are prudes, too... check."

"I wasn't always a New Yorker." She hit him, a gentle swat upside the arm. "If I had a glass of wine or three, I wouldn't care if you joked about the hairs growing out of your ass, but when you're telling me everything could come to an end if some vampires up in space don't protect us, well, I'm not sure how to take that."

"None of us are." He rubbed his arm with a half-smile, then said, "I'm sorry. The Force de Guerre, FDG I mean, we all just know it so it doesn't seem like a big deal."

"Well, Valerie mentioned something that Michael had said about all this, so it's not out of nowhere. It's just... When you hear it from two sources, it's different."

They sat there for a moment, each lost in thought, until the scent of the croissants brought Sandra back to the moment. She stood and found two plates, then served a croissant to him and sat down with her own. It was still hot enough that, when she bit into it, the layers collapsed onto the chocolate and steam came out.

And oh, my, God, was it delicious. Flaky, chocolaty goodness filled her mouth and senses, overwhelming her so that she was barely able to hear the moans coming from Garcia.

"The fuck is this?" a voice said, and a moment later the door opened to reveal Diego. His face was pale, eyes wide with confusion.

"Yo," Garcia said, wiping chocolate from his mouth. "How the hell do you stay so thin with your wife cooking it up like this?"

The red of Diego's cheeks returned as he processed the man in front of him. "Oh, damn, I... I heard moaning and..."

Sandra sat her croissant down and turned to him, arms folded. "Excuse me? You thought what, that I might be having an affair?"

He grimaced.

"Trust me, mate," Garcia said. "If she were having an affair, it wouldn't be with me. I'm too tall."

"Freakishly," Diego said, striding forward to give the man an embrace. "It's good to see you, really, but I can't focus until I have one of those croissants in my belly."

So he joined them, and Sandra was certain any passersby would think they were having a ménage a trois in here. But, as Garcia went on to explain the situation to Diego now, Sandra couldn't help but think about two things. The first was that, he was right—though it wasn't about short or tall, it was about Diego. He was her type now, no one else. And the second was that, while they'd never been married, Diego didn't correct the man when he had called her Diego's wife.

CHAPTER FIVE

On the Air Ships

Sunrise had already hit as Valerie heaved Royland over the side railing and into the blimp. He grunted from the short fall onto the deck. She had kept him in the shadows, so the sun couldn't touch him. A moment later, she had climbed over to join him.

"Hurry and heal, would you?" she said, glancing around at the shapes of men and women who had apparently not noticed their arrival yet.

Robin crouched down beside them under cover of several crates of supplies, her two swords at the ready.

Valerie glanced down at Royland and decided it was best to give him another vial of blood. "Don't worry, we'll have plenty of chances to fill these up in the next few minutes," she said as she pressed a vial to his lips.

He was already looking better, and this time took the vial for himself and drank.

"The hell happened?" she hissed, holding her hand up to tell Robin to give her a minute.

He finished the blood, gave her the vial, and then breathed in deep before forcing a smile.

"I jumped."

It took her a moment to process what he had said, but then she just laughed. "That explains why you're all beat up. Not that it makes sense."

"They had her in the other blimp, I thought I could make it." He sat up now, leaning against the crates, and turned his head to see Robin. "Who's the new girl?"

"Right, you two haven't met yet. How about we take this ship, and then commence with introductions?"

He nodded. "Not sure how much help I'll be."

"Don't get killed," she said with a laugh. "That's all I can ask for."

"I can do that."

"Cammie would kick my ass if she found out I let you die." Valerie motioned to Robin to move forward. "Well, try anyway."

"She's grown more vicious since you left," he said. "Just... better keep me alive."

"Guess we'll see what happens."

She glanced over to see Robin at the edge of the crates, a pirate running past and toward the captain's cabin in a rush.

The man never even saw the assassin coming. Quick as a flash, Robin was at his side, one sword in his gut the other under his throat. She lifted both and used them to propel him over the side of the blimp, his throat slit so that no sound came as he fell.

Valerie had to nod with respect at that move. This Robin girl didn't have half the power she did, but that didn't stop her from being a regular badass.

Now it was Valerie's turn. Two pirates were pulling in the ropes on the far side of the ship, so she charged them. Figuring she would keep her blade clean, she simply slammed their heads together and then tossed them over the side to join their fallen comrade below.

She spun at a creak in the wooden deck, only to see Robin standing there, glancing over the side after the bodies.

"How many do we need alive to catch the other blimp?" Robin asked.

"The captain," Valerie replied. "All we have to do is catch her, not land this balloon."

Robin frowned.

"You do realize they're pirates?" Valerie asked. "Cutthroats, men and women who steal from us... and enslave people."

"Fuck you." Robin held up one of her bloody swords. "They're people, and we don't know their full story."

Valerie was about to argue, when she thought back to Jackson and how, when she had met him, he had been on the other side. A lot of people in Old Manhattan had taken their turns on various sides, but that didn't make them all bad.

"Dammit," Valerie said. "Fine, we don't kill the ones we don't have to. But if they try to kill us or stand in our way...?"

"Slice 'em ear to ear," Robin said. "Don't worry about me. All I gotta do is imagine them forcing my parents to do hard labor, and I'm just like you."

"Just like me?"

"A killing machine." Robin's eyes went wide at Valerie's expression. "That bothers you? You're actually bothered that I see you this way?"

"I wasn't always like this." Valerie turned from Robin, horrified that this was the image she now represented. "Conditions have forced me into this role."

"Ladies," a hiss came from Royland's direction. He was kneeling now, appearing to have healed quickly. "Maybe this conversation can wait until after we've rescued Cammie?"

"Your broken friend has a point," Robin said.

"It's Royland," he said, then nodded toward the captain's tower.

"Robin," she said back with a nod.

"Now that we got that out of the way..." Valerie nodded to Robin, pulling out her sword this time.

The two ran over to the captain's cabin, while Royland mumbled something about keeping watch in the back.

"One of your lovers?" Robin asked with a playful smile.

Valerie stood at the door that led in, prepared to kick it in. "Oddly, I've never been with a vampire," she said, only pausing long enough to note the intrigued expression on Robin's face before charging in.

The door flew open with a bang and, unlike the last time she'd charged into a cabin like this, a line of pirates was waiting. They held their weapons at the ready, and once they had processed what was happening, opened fire with shotguns, rifles, pistols, and some small darts that stung like a bitch.

Valerie's first instinct was to throw herself over Robin, but Robin pushed her off and charged even as flesh burst from her as bullets ripped through her body.

A metal net shot out and almost had her, but she swiped it aside with her swords. The move left her exposed, though, and a pirate pushed in with a metal glove. He caught her in the stomach and, to Valerie's surprise, Robin collapsed to the floor.

This wasn't going to plan at all, so Valerie decided a different approach was in order. As a bullet hit her in the calf and she cursed, she rolled past them so that one of the pirates turned to shoot at her but ended up strafing a couple of his buddies.

When they collapsed, Valerie had come up behind the others and, in spite of the oh-so-annoying pain tearing through her, commenced with ripping those sons of bitches to shreds with her sword.

Blood splattered the walls and window. Bodies covered the floor. Only one of them was left—the captain.

Valerie took a step toward him, about to tell him not to move, when Robin lunged, screaming, blood dripping from holes in her body, and she tore his throat out in one quick motion, sinking her teeth into him to consume his blood.

The wounds were already starting to heal by the time she dropped his lifeless corpse to the ground.

Valerie stared in shock, paused to fill up her two empty vials, and then assessed her friend.

"Are you... feeling better?"

Robin looked up at her from where she sat on the ground in a puddle of blood. "Why'd you save me?"

"What?"

"Back there, at the Black Plague headquarters," Robin replied. "You could've just let me die. You could've ended this pain, let it all slip away, and let me rest in peace."

"You'd prefer to die and leave your parents as slaves, never knowing what happened to you?"

"As if they'd rather know I became this?!" Robin stood, shuddered in pain and nearly slipped in the blood that pooled on the floor, then gestured to herself. "I'm a fucking monster!"

Valerie stepped forward, very conscious of the pain in her leg, and wrapped her arms around the girl. "You're not a monster, you're just a woman who will do anything to save her parents. And a woman who's strong enough to see that through."

Robin clutched at Valerie, pulling her close, head on her shoulder, and then looked up. Where Valerie had expected to see tears, Robin's eyes were hard, committed.

"You're right." Robin pulled back, checking some of the smaller wounds that had healed. "Maybe this isn't a curse at all. Maybe I've been turned into the ultimate weapon, the tool necessary to bring those slavers down."

"To bring them justice." Valerie assured her. "And I'll be at your side, tearing them all new assholes."

"We all will be," Royland's voice came from the doorway. "Assuming we save Cammie, that is. Based on what I'm seeing here, I have no idea how that's possible."

"No one here knows how to fly one of these?" Valerie asked.

"I had a bicycle, once," Robin offered, with a frown. "Who is this Cammie to you?"

"Everything," Royland replied with a nod to the control booth. At the front of the captain's cabin, a small wall of knobs and buttons sat unoccupied, along with a metal rod sticking up in the middle. "You're our best bet, it looks like."

Robin laughed and then seeing that he wasn't joking, bit her lip and was at the controls in three painful strides.

"Can you figure it out?" Valerie asked.

"Don't see how I have a choice," Robin replied. "It's that, or we'll never find out where the rest of the pirates are, we'll never find my parents, and we'll never be able to re-unite him with his everything."

Royland stepped up beside her, but it was clear he had no idea how the controls worked.

"I watched a captain sail one of these, once," Valerie offered. "When I first flew over from Old France."

She stepped up and moved the stick. Sure enough, they began to veer left.

"There we go," Royland said.

Valerie smiled, then looked for the way to accelerate. "Any ideas here?"

Royland pressed one button, and the whole ship shuddered. "Not doing that one again." He was about to press a large, round one when Robin grabbed his hand.

"Wait…" She pointed at a handle next to numbers one through five, and then moved the handle to the next highest number.

Sure enough, the blimp lurched forward and then began to pick up speed.

"I like your new friend," Royland said to Valerie. "Smart. Resourceful."

Robin grunted. "And you don't seem like the complete jackoff Valerie says a lot of vampires are."

"You said that?" Royland asked Valerie.

"We have a lot of good ones," Valerie answered. "But it's mostly true. Imagine how many I've killed since I started this quest, and how many more we'll have to take down before this is over. I don't know if it's a case of power corrupting, or if it's that they believe the legends and that they have to live up to them. Regardless, most vampires are dicks."

He chuckled, clutching a wound in his stomach that hadn't fully healed. "I know I was, before you all came along and saved me from the blood banks."

"The blood banks?" Robin asked.

Valerie nodded, glancing out through the blood-smeared window to see how far off the other blimp was. They were gaining on it.

"When we first took Old Manhattan," she explained, "the top dogs there were using Weres to hunt vampires, then draining them of their blood and selling it on the black market."

"That's... wow."

"It's supposedly addictive as hell," Royland interjected. "And keeps its drinkers healthier... maybe younger, but I'm not sure."

"And you were one of these vampires?"

Royland nodded. "Used to be what some circles call a Forsaken. Had my own clan and nosferatu and everything, even a few people who thought we were gods and let us feed on them."

Valerie noticed Robin's eyes narrowing as he talked, so she cut in. "But ever since that day, he's been one of my most trusted friends. And more than that to Cammie, who would have kicked my ass if we'd left him behind for the sun to get."

"Speaking of the sun," he said, and inched in from the doorway where the sunlight was just now starting to reach forward. He closed the door and leaned against it. "How're we going to fight them when only you can go out there?"

Valerie motioned to Robin, and said, "We're evolving. Well, not actually, but on our trip to Chicago we found Robin and others who had come up with clothing that helps them move in the sun."

"Scary as hell," Robin interjected, pulling her mask on so he could see. "But it works."

"But you look like a ninja." He chuckled. "I mean, it's kinda funny, right? Ninjas and pirates... What's next? People are going to start throwing fire from their hands or control the shadows with their minds?"

Valerie cocked her head, curious. "It's not so impossible, is it?"

"What?" He scoffed. "Explain."

"Well, that night when I met Michael, it was like... like he was controlling lightning."

Royland pursed his lips. "And you can kinda read minds."

"You can do what?" Robin said, turning on Valerie now. "How dare you. If you so much as peeked into my—"

"Whoa, whoa!" Valerie held up her hands to hold off the advancing woman. "No, it's not exactly like he said. I can sense emotions, in a way. If you're sad, or maybe if you're about to attack me. Stuff like that."

"And don't forget about pushing fear," Royland said.

"Yes, and that. Thank you, Royland."

"I'm familiar with that one," Robin said with a chuckle.

Valerie assumed she was thinking back to the fight at Black Plague headquarters, but thought it best not to linger there.

Instead, she turned her attention back to the other blimp, which they were quickly approaching.

"Why aren't they running?" Robin asked.

"They don't know we've taken over," Royland replied. "Far as they know, we're just their fellow pirates who also escaped the chaos below."

"Damn. That's going to come as a shock for them."

"Robin and I will make the jump when we're close enough

but…" Valerie started, but then saw movement on the front of the ship, followed by a body flying overboard. "Holy shit."

Royland nodded, a broad smile on his face. "That's my girl, er, don't tell her I said that."

"What is it?" Robin said, trying to get a view but was obstructed by the eye-covers in her mask. They let her see, but it was tough—it had to be, in order to keep the sun out.

"Looks like it won't be as much of a rescue mission as a help-her-out mission," Valerie said, drawing her sword again. "Ready?"

Robin nodded.

"Royland, keep her close," Valerie said, and then the two charged.

CHAPTER SIX

On the Air Ships

The damn metal ropes had cut bad gashes into her flesh, but Cammie hadn't let that stop her. Any normal person would have given up in the face of such pain, but not her.

She had struggled against the ropes, pushing and swinging until she had managed to get to the base of them, the part that was cinched together and made of leather, and then her nails had done their job.

A few minutes of hanging on for dear life as the winds whipped her hair about her face, and then she was climbing up, gripping on for dear life as blood soaked into her shirt. By the time she had reached the side of the ship, her wounds were already healing.

Her desire for vengeance, however, was in full swing.

That was why, when she saw a pirate turn with wide, horrified eyes, she leapt without a second thought. He tried to dig his thumbs into the remnants of her wounds, but she was too busy digging her thumbs into his eyes to care. Adrenaline pumped through her body as she tossed him aside, still screaming.

Good, she thought. They'll hear it and come running.

And she was ready for them, now in full wolf form. These dickwads had fucked with the wrong Were. She charged around their attacks, tearing out calves and biting into groins, pulling and spraying blood. The deck grew slick, and she continued the fight.

One came at her with a makeshift spear and she dodged, only to see that it had some sort of contraption on it that exploded, knocking her to the deck.

She twisted out of the way as shots rang out, then sprang back up and was at it again. A figure appeared behind her and she turned to attack, but froze—Valerie?

Sure enough, it was Valerie and a figure dressed in black from head to toe.

"We got you," Valerie said, then turned her red, glowing eyes back to the attackers.

This just went from revenge pissed-off to revenge this-will-be-fun. In the spirit of excitement, Cammie transformed back into a nude woman, having dropped her clothes when transforming the first time.

It was enough to distract the charging pirates, and was damn funny when one of those pirates had been mid-run, missed a step, slipped in the blood, and went flying overboard.

"Just keep showing 'em your bush and we don't have to fight," Valerie said with a smirk. "Odd, how it makes them flee though, isn't it?"

"Oh shut up," Cammie said, not even bothering to dress as she tore through the female pirate who hadn't been distracted and continued to press the attack. "Royland has no complaints."

"That man's addicted to Cammie," Valerie said with a laugh. "No question about it."

"What's up with the ninja princess?" Cammie asked, tossing the pirate aside and glancing back at the one clad all in black.

"I prefer Robin," the ninja lady said, clutching two swords and standing at the ready. "In case you didn't know, you're naked."

"Yes, the wind is cold as fuck on my nipples, so…" Cammie pursed her lips, motioning toward the group of pirates now forming a semi-circle around them, debating their next move.

"No bickering, children," Valerie said, and then she stepped forward into the attack. She brought her sword up in a strike, and the battle was back on… but not for long. Soon, pirates were running and trying to make it for the other blimp, apparently not putting it together that the two newcomers had come from there.

When only two remained on deck, Cammie turned back to get dressed, letting Valerie and Robin deal with them. She was mad about losing her cowboy hat, and now that she looked down at where her clothes had fallen, she was pissed to see the shirt was covered with blood.

At first, she debated simply going shirtless, but the wind was damn cold, after all. She glanced around and saw that one of the two survivors was a woman of about her size, wearing a black hat that had some similarities to her old one, with a turquoise feather on it. She wore a dress to match, with what looked like a corset around her waist and frills coming out the back in a way that reminded Cammie of a peacock.

"Hold on," Cammie said, covering herself from the wind as she walked back over. She looked the woman pirate up and down, then said, "Are you evil?"

"What?" the woman hissed, wild eyes darting back and forth between her and Valerie.

"Are you a bad person? Do you steal? Would you slit our throats while we sleep? You get the gist."

The pirate focused her eyes on her and spat out, "I'll tear out your tongue and gouge out your eyes, you miserable horse's ass. The hell kind of question is that? I'm a damn pirate, you understand? Lady Death, they call me back in Toro, because I'll fucking bring the—"

CRACK. Cammie moved in a quick motion, snapping the woman's neck so as to avoid blood on her new clothes.

"What was all that about?" Robin asked, and Cammie wished she could see the woman's face under that mask to tell if she was asking in the judgmental way it sounded like.

"Makes me sleep better at night if I know the person I kill would've done the same to me," Cammie replied, and began undressing the woman.

"And you're stealing her clothes…"

Cammie began to slide the dress off the woman, but paused to look at Robin. "It's probably something we should all consider doing, if we want to do any sort of undercover work. Plus, I think my man will find it sexy as hell."

"No doubts there," Valerie interjected, standing next to the captain's door. "That said, we still have this to deal with, and it sounds like there's more than one of them in there. If you're worried about blood on the new dress."

"You like the nude look on me, Val?" Cammie chuckled. "All this time, you coulda just asked."

Valerie turned away, actually blushing. This was too much. Cammie stood, holding the dress in one hand, breasts warmed by the orange glow of sunrise.

"Is there something going on here that I don't know about?" she asked, stepping toward Valerie while doing her best to conceal a smile. "Because… you know my pack from before was very open to the idea of more than one woman in a man's bed. I could talk to Royland, see if he's interested. Can't see why he wouldn't be."

"Cammie, we're dealing with something here," Valerie said, refusing to turn and look at her.

"I'm sure they'd all like to hear your thoughts on the matter." Cammie strode forward, licking her lips, when suddenly Robin was in her path.

"Enough."

"What's wrong, new girl doesn't like all the fun?" Cammie was about to make another comment, when she noticed the woman's mask was tilted down toward her chest. "You know, just because you're wearing a mask doesn't mean I can't tell you're checking me out."

"Enough!" Robin said, her right sword twitching.

Cammie cocked her head in a try me sort of way, and then realization dawned. "Is... is there something going on between the two of you?"

"No," Valerie said, finally turning to glare at her. "And you're starting to make me wish we'd just left you here to die."

"In case you hadn't noticed, I was on my way to taking down the entire crew on my own."

"Will you put a damn shirt on so we can walk in there and kill us some pirates?"

Cammie took a step back, not used to Valerie raising her voice like that. "Yeah, I imagine Royland is waiting anxiously."

"He is." Valerie looked between Robin and Cammie, then said, "Do we have a problem?" When neither replied, Valerie said, "Good," and then kicked in the door to the control room.

Cammie cursed, stowed the dress and hat behind the corner in hopes that the wind would leave them be, and followed Robin in after Valerie. She immediately wished she had at least put a shirt on, because in the cabin were twin boys who looked to be no older than fourteen, an older girl in a pretty, white dress, and the man who she assumed was the captain. He held a crossbow out, aimed at them, but instead of a normal crossbow bolt, the contraption looked like a bronze-grenade at the end of a stick.

"Step any closer and we all die," the captain said.

"Cover your eyes," the girl mumbled to the boys, leading Cammie to assume she was their older sister. The girl held her hand to her mouth, as if sure she was about to die for opening it.

"Nothing wrong with seeing a pair of amazing tits," Cammie said, stepping forward and baring her claws. "At least they got something before they died."

"We got lots of somethings," one of the boys said, his eyes

nowhere near reaching up to her face, "if that's what somethings means."

Cammie paused, glanced over at the sweating captain, and said, "I like this one. He can live."

The others went pale, but Robin said, "They all live." She took off her mask then and gave Valerie a glance that said she was serious as hell. She turned to Cammie. "Will you put some clothes on and shut up?"

Cammie blinked, caught off guard, first by the comment, and second at the realization that this girl was barely a woman at all. Her dark hair was pulled into a pony tail behind her, but was fairly short, and her high cheekbones and pale skin gave her a very young, traditional vampire look.

"Robin, that's my friend you're talking to, so be nice." Valerie glanced over her shoulder and said, "And Cammie, go put some fucking clothes on."

The up-to-now silent boy gasped, and she turned back to him. "You can't be serious. You're pirate kids and you gasp at swearing?"

"For your information," the girl said, pulling at her brother to keep him close, her eyes wide with fright, "We weren't pirate kids, not until a few days ago, anyway."

Cammie wanted to hear this, but out of respect for Valerie, glanced around and found a pirate captain's hat, which she used to cover her chest.

"Explain," she said.

Valerie and Robin waited, but the girl looked too terrified to say another word, so the captain stepped forward.

"You may not remember me...." he started, but suddenly Valerie gasped and said, "Captain Bronson?"

He nodded, eyes staring at her cautiously.

"But... but you went back to Europe," she continued. "To your family, to... Oh, shit. You never went back, did you?"

He shook his head. "I wanted to, more than anything. But

after losing our cargo, and then a couple of big runs I tried to make fell through, and one guy didn't pay up, well... this is where they threw me. When they learned I could captain ships and blimps, I found my place, and they didn't kill me. Always wondered if they would, but they never did."

"And then...?"

"They came looking for me." He sniffled, looking at his children with such adoration, Cammie wasn't sure if she'd ever seen that look in someone's eyes. "I'm a piece of shit—sorry kids, but it's true—for leaving them. I thought I could make enough to return and provide for them, but once I was here, the pirates wouldn't let me leave."

"I don't understand," Robin said. "The pirates, they let you keep your children?"

He nodded. "I was bringing them back to The Isle of the Prince, promised that if I could leave my kids with a friend there, I'd take these jackholes on the biggest score run of their lives."

"Old Manhattan," Valerie said, knowingly. "You told them you knew its ins and outs."

"You got that part right, but what you ain't got is the part about my plan to run once we hit the Isle of the Prince. No matter what, we'd be done with this place."

Robin held up a hand. "You're still not connecting the dots, mister. See, thing is, you just said these three kids found you. How the hell do I process that? Found you here...?"

"And you said they were in Europe," Valerie interjected. "If I remember correctly."

He nodded, but his daughter was the one who answered. "Mom passed away, we had nowhere else to go. Took us six months before we found him."

"Holy shit," Cammie said.

"Language, please," Captain Bronson said, earning him a snarl, but when Valerie glanced Cammie's way, she backed down. Apparently they knew each other, and she didn't yet know to what degree. Hell, it was possible she was more loyal to this guy than to Cammie.

"Fine, language," Cammie turned to the kids. "I gotta know, how'd you survive out here? How'd you make the trip? How...?" She took a whiff, then groaned. "I can't believe I didn't notice it before. Which one of you?"

They all looked at each other, then looked to the ground, all but the one who had gasped at swearing.

"Seriously?" she asked.

In response, his eyes glowed yellow and he showed sharp, wolf teeth.

"Weres can't partially transform," Robin said, confusion creasing her brow. "Everyone knows that."

"It's rare," Cammie said, repeating the partial transformation to prove her point. "I've only ever met one other who could do it, and he's standing right in front of us."

"But... he's... how come they're not, I mean you're not all Weres then."

Captain Bronson shrugged. "As far as I knew, their mother wasn't—"

"She was, Dad," the boy said. "She showed me, after she realized what I was."

"To be clear," the other boy said, raising his hand. "You're not going to try and kill us?"

"Try?" Valerie asked with a chuckle. "Honey, if we tried, you'd be dead."

He shrugged. "My brother has taken on worse than you."

This time, Valerie had to laugh out loud. "I doubt there is such a thing as worse than us, at least not in this part of the world, right now."

"You didn't answer the question," he reminded her.

Valerie turned to Cammie and Robin with a raised eyebrow. "Thoughts? Should we kill them?"

Robin rolled her eyes. "Ignore them," she said to the kid.

"They're playing, but the answer's a solid no. We're not the type to run around killing without reason, or enslaving people… or abandoning people."

"So what do you have in mind?" the sister asked.

"We're going to help you," Valerie said, kneeling next to them. "I trust your father, and maybe I shouldn't trust kids nowadays, but I do."

"We're not kids," the girl said. "They're fourteen, and I'm sixteen."

"Good for you."

"We have a destination in mind then?" Cammie asked. "This Isle of the Prince? Because, as fun as this is, I want to put on my new clothes and go over to the other blimp. Royland's probably pretty damn curious about what happened, and as anxious as I am to be together again."

"Is that a sexual reference?" the non-Were boy asked.

"Someone give this kid a private bathroom for fifteen minutes." She turned and left them to it, then found her newly acquired pirate clothes. It took a moment to figure out how to put them on, but then she was dressed and placed the hat upon her head.

She felt good, and knew for a fact that she looked damn good.

Royland better damn well say so.

At the blimp's edge, she waved over to the control room and a moment later saw the blimp veer their way.

"Whoa, whoa!" she said as the other blimp nearly collided with theirs, the two balloons barely scraping against each other. A bit more and there could have been a major disaster.

"Sorry!" Royland called out, appearing in the shadowed portion of the doorway to the control room on the opposite ship. "Still getting used to this."

"Hold her steady!" Cammie shouted, and prepared to jump.

"Cammie!" Valerie called out, jogging over. "Be careful, you hear me?"

"We'll follow close," Cammie said. "What's the destination?"

"This island they speak of. Follow the coast northwest, and you can't miss it, or so I'm told. But you also can't miss us."

"Gotcha." Cammie prepared to jump again, then said, "And if we can't figure out how to land that thing?"

"You join us here, but… why not just do it now anyway? Abandon the other blimp."

Cammie smiled. "Because I'm thinking Royland and I need a bit of alone time to celebrate our joyous reunion."

"I don't need the details," Valerie said with a grin. "Just make him shout loud enough for us to hear over here, and we'll know you did it right."

"I've never done it any other way," Cammie said, and then she ran, turquoise dress trailing behind her, and jumped. For a moment, nothing but air was beneath her, then a sight of hills and valleys. Then her feet hit the far deck and she rolled with a thud, slamming her head up against the control panel.

"I'd come out and help," Royland said, "but this whole dying in the sunlight business puts a damper on that."

"You stay right there." Cammie pushed herself up, leaning on the wall for support, and then said, "We're going to make up for a bit of lost time."

"You mean… that little, tiny bit of time just now?"

"Yeah, but I believe in interest. Large amounts of it." With a wide smile, and feeling sexy as hell in her new outfit, she sauntered in after him. The door hadn't even closed behind her yet when she had begun pulling his clothes off.

CHAPTER SEVEN

New York

Sandra led Diego and Garcia along an attractive walkway with small trees growing on one side that had been transplanted from what was once Central Park, and a small stream flowing gently down the other.

"The city has moved light-years ahead toward improvement," Diego explained to their guest. "When we arrived, people lived in fear. Medical supplies were in short supply, and the city was divided into factions that were fighting turf wars."

"And now?"

"Valerie cleaned it up," Sandra said.

"Valerie, Sandra, Colonel Donnoly, and all the rest," Diego corrected her. "The people willing to make a change have started stepping forward, and some have even set up neighborhood watches."

"And you're talking all of this in, what? Half a year?" Garcia whistled. "Not bad."

"Less, actually."

"What?"

Diego smiled. "Less. More like a couple months."

"How the hell… Ah, right, Valerie."

With a finger held up, Diego again said, "And Sandra, Colonel Donnoly, me—"

"Yes, we get the idea," Sandra said with a laugh. "Thanks, dear."

"And these factions, they're gone completely?" Garcia asked.

Diego shrugged. "It's hard to say for sure. They haven't shown their faces, but it's such a short amount of time."

"We'll have to watch out for that," he said. "The worst kind of war one can fight is from within."

"Trust me," Sandra interjected, "we've had more than our fair share of internal war. If there's a higher power, I'd say they owe us a break."

"But you've seen what lies between here and Chicago, right?" Garcia took the steps to the dirt path below, ears perking at shouting in the distance—the shouting of men and women training. "It ain't pretty out there."

"I'm just glad we don't have to clean it up all by ourselves," Sandra replied. "Remind me to send TH a box of chocolates, would you?"

"Sure thing," Garcia said with a wink.

They crested a hill and came to the point in the park where they could look out over the vampires and Weres training. They had finished hand-to-hand now, and some were traversing an obstacle course they had made just a week earlier, while others were moving to the vacated buildings nearby to practice insurgent strategies.

"This ain't bad," Garcia said with a huge grin, tucking his thumbs into his belt loops. "A bit sloppy over there," he pointed to the way some of the Weres were moving into the building, "leaving themselves open like that. But overall, I'd say we have some mighty-fine clay to work with."

"Well, let's get you in there then, and introduce you to the guys," Sandra said.

Diego shook his head, biting his lip.

"Yes?"

"Don't you think we should check in with Donnoly first?" Diego asked. "I mean, I know he's not in charge of this, per se, but he is charged with internal security. Bringing in someone from the outside and just letting him in like this…"

"You don't trust me?" Garcia asked. "No, I get it. For all you know, I might have been kicked out for something horrible. I could've come here with this story, only to do something horrible again."

"Did you?" Sandra asked.

He shook his head. "Of course not, but I get his concern."

Sandra gave Diego a reproachful look. "He did help us take down the CEOs."

"And I'm a super nice guy."

"Right. And he's a super nice guy."

Diego pursed his lips, unsure.

"Honestly, I'm in no rush," Garcia said. "You take me to meet this Donnoly character, and I can get cleaned up. Then we have a nice chat about how best to make this happen. TH was specific on us needing to partner, but didn't want to force you all into anything you weren't comfortable with."

"Works for me." Diego shrugged. "But only because we had croissants together."

"The key to all great partnerships." Garcia rubbed his belly. "Good thing there aren't more of those in my part of the world, or I'd have a hard time on those obstacle courses."

"You can do them?"

He shook his head. "Not exactly. In fact, I don't think I ever have. But real combat? You bet your boots I can do that."

Diego glanced down at his boots, an old black pair with yellow laces.

"How about I bet you another round of croissants that you can't do the course as fast as me."

"Right now?"

Diego nodded.

"Accepted," Garcia said, and took off at a jog.

Diego hesitated, glancing back at Sandra, then smiled and said, "Sorry, dear, I can't let him win."

"Just go," she said, waving him off, and she started trekking down the hill as he took off in a jog.

Boys.

She laughed, realizing she'd probably be running over there right now, too, if not for the baby growing inside of her. As she walked to catch up with them, she had a thought that troubled her. How many babies had she seen in the city? The answer was a simple one. Zero. None.

Just another confirmation that the events that had brought about the Great Collapse had also affected people's ability to reproduce.

The thought made her both appreciative of her current situation, and deeply concerned for the survival of the human race.

With the amount of violence, how long could the world survive if humanity continued to grow at such a low rate as she imagined must be the case?

Reaching the edge of the training ground, she sat on a fallen tree and watched Diego and Garcia making their way through the obstacle course. Diego was clearly faster, but when he stopped to taunt the soldier, Garcia tackled him, put him in an arm-bar, and then laughed before running to get a head start on the wall ahead of them.

Sandra chuckled to herself as Diego stood, brushed himself off, and gestured angrily at him, clearly saying something but too far off for her to hear.

"Suck it up and kick his butt, honey!" she shouted, waving him on.

A pod pulled up between her and the course at that moment. The early sunlight glinted off of the window, causing her to have to look away to avoid the glare, but when she looked again, she saw Presley and Esmerelda step out, followed by Colonel Donnoly. The hell were the three of them doing together, she wondered, though she didn't have to stretch her mind far too figure it out—especially when Presley gave him a playful cup of the sac that she thought no one else could see.

To his credit, he brushed her hand away and glanced around, nervously. He was the commander of the police, so had to keep it professional.

His eyes came to rest on her sitting there, and he smiled, his cheeks flushing red enough to be visible from where she sat.

"The troops pulling through?" he asked as he approached.

She stood and he waved her to stay seated, but she said, "No, I need to keep moving. Gotta stay in shape for when this whole thing happens." She rubbed her belly and grinned. "The troops are looking good, and I'm glad you're here."

"Is that abnormal?"

She laughed. "I mean exceptionally glad. See that man there?" She pointed to Garcia.

"The man your hubby is trouncing?"

She nodded, cocking her head. "Since when did this become a husband and wife situation?"

"What?"

"It's just… Nothing." She shook it off, wondering if Diego had started referring to her as his wife or something. "We need to talk."

The two strolled back down toward the troops, a new group of them running past, as she told him about Garcia and why he was there. She was looking out across the troops, all Weres and normal humans now, because the vampires had to retreat to their barracks during the day. They'd set up two defensive positions, one up here, and another on the southwest edge of the city.

Brad had tried to convince her to force them to train during the day as well, with their protective gear on, but both she and

Colonel Donnoly agreed that was a bad idea. One mistake could end with the death of one of their most powerful soldiers, if the clothing moved with friction or fighting, exposing them to the sun.

Still, he had a point, so she had told him to practice carefully for the first hour each evening with the sunset.

"I don't know if I like it," Donnoly said after she had finished explaining Garcia's role here, and their potential partnership with TH and the FDG. "You all might have met this TH, but I haven't."

"Shouldn't my say so be enough?"

"Yes, it probably should… But it's not." He glanced back at the sergeant, who was shaking hands with Diego now, having been beaten. He might be a badass, but Diego was her man. Her Were man.

"I'll take him under my wing, vouch for him."

"You?" Donnoly's eyes automatically dropped to her belly, but she scoffed.

"Excuse me. This baby won't be coming for a few months still. By then, everything will be in place. At least you'll know then if you can trust him or not."

A group of Weres ran by, led by one of the large ones who had come with the group from the Golden City, and she nodded at his salute. Taking up the rear, two Weres were glaring at her. She did a double take, but they weren't looking anymore, and she wondered if she'd imagined it.

"Get it done," Donnoly said.

She nodded as he returned to his ladies, and she returned to Diego and Garcia. This was going to be fun. At least they were at peace for now, and she was safe. She hoped the same could be said for Valerie.

CHAPTER EIGHT

On the Air Ships

Valerie had done her best to ignore the rocking of the other blimp as they rode along, but the constant course corrections as their autopilot setup failed them was harder to ignore. More than once, Captain Bronson had to steer clear of the other blimp, cursing.

They sat in his cabin, while the kids were cleaning up outside. Valerie had found an outfit of black with a gold corset and hat to match, and Robin had on a violet pirate dress, though she still had to wear her mask and assassin clothes, too, during the sunlight hours.

"You're sure about bringing kids into a pirate city?" Valerie asked.

Bronson shook his head. "Not at all, but the only other option is to turn around and head back to Old Manhattan. Something tells me you wouldn't like that."

"We need you," she said. "You, and the blimp will help us get to Toro. We'll need you to fly."

He scoffed, but then seemed to think about it and said, "Keep us safe, here and when we go back to the city, right?"

He wouldn't need her help, not if he was arriving with a family, but decided she didn't need to know that right now. "Deal."

"The kids have fended for themselves up to now, but, never again, if I can help it."

Valerie shared a look of understanding with him, then turned back to watch the other blimp start to turn toward them again.

"Come on! Will someone go over there and steer it for them?" Bronson shouted. "For the love of…" He paused at what sounded like screams, turned back with a frightened look, and then frowned. "Dammit!"

"You hear a scream nowadays, you immediately leap to thoughts of death and destruction." Valerie nodded, staring out the window at the other blimp as it once again jerked to the right. The sun was passing its zenith in the sky now, making the other blimp gleam and casting a blinding light from the window. "I get that, but when you're in the same vicinity as Cammie, that's not always the case."

Bronson smiled, but had a far-off look in his eyes. "That's a scream I haven't heard for some time."

"Wife was hard to please?" Robin asked, sitting in the corner and picking her nails with one of her swords.

"What? No," he laughed. "God, no. She was a squealer though, never a screamer."

"TMI, for sure," Valerie said, shooting a glare in Robin's direction.

"What?" Robin smiled and raised an eyebrow. "A girl can be curious. This whole thing… it's out of my area of expertise."

Valerie bit her lip at the images that statement put through her mind, but shook it off.

"I meant," Bronson continued, "it has been a while since, you know, with my wife. Now that she's passed… who knows."

"Luckily, your kids are occupied," Valerie said, turning to see out through the doorway that the kids had finished scrubbing the deck. "Good way to build character, I guess. Having kids mop up blood."

"In this world?" Bronson laughed a mirthless laugh. "They'll be doing much worse than that if they hope to survive."

"Not in the Manhattan we're establishing," Valerie said. "They used to call it New York, right? Well, it'll be new again, soon enough." She chuckled. "New York… if the city truly understands all that went into that name now."

"It won't last," Bronson said. "It never does."

"You don't know that."

"America… what used to be America, it's too big. Too spread out. There's no army that could keep peace, and too many crazies out there to allow it."

"We met someone," Valerie argued, "A man who I think will make all the difference."

"He's got a charming smile they'll all flock to?" Bronson scoffed. "A golden cock? I wanna know how he bewitched you into believing this was possible."

Valerie snapped her fingers, and he turned to look at her. For a moment, she let her eyes flash red. "You talk like that around your children, fine. But insinuate bullshit like that about me again, your kids will be orphans."

"I didn't mean…"

"Yes. You did." She held his gaze a moment longer, letting him know she wouldn't take disrespect. "For your information, this guy and I never did anything like that. His woman, Char, certainly wouldn't have been too keen on that."

"The Were?" Robin asked. "Ah, this Terry Henry Walton character, yeah."

"And he is?" Bronson asked.

"He's set up an army, out of Chicago. The Force De Guerre, or FDG, he calls them. If we pull together, join forces… it might be possible."

Bronson frowned. "Yeah, I've heard that name. He or his guys,

I don't know, they were associated with bringing a certain amount of order to Old Manhattan, a while back. But... I thought he was super old. He can't still be alive."

"He is."

"A vampire?" Bronson frowned. "I don't believe it. That would've gotten out... right?"

"Not a vampire. He's been modified, but, no, I don't think you would say he's a vampire."

Robin cocked her head. "Can you... speak English?"

Valerie laughed. "Modified, like, the way I understand it anyway, me and you were. Our blood has something in it, and that's what makes us who we are. Similar with Weres, and there's some other form of this out there—modified humans who wouldn't really fall under either category." She shrugged. "I guess, I mean, it's not like I quizzed him about it much. I was too busy loving that steak dinner they gave us before we left."

Robin smiled and licked her lips. "I could eat like that every night and never get bored of it."

"True, but the world would run out of cows," Valerie replied. "I'll see what I can do, for you."

Bronson noticed the smile and the look between the two. "So... not experienced in that area, huh?" he asked Robin.

She frowned, not getting it, then frowned more when she did. "None of your business."

He turned his smile to Valerie, but when he saw her eyes flash red, he quickly turned back to the controls, staring out the window.

"Dad!" his daughter said, running in through the door. "The island, I see it."

Valerie ran outside with her, Robin following while throwing her mask back on. They stood at the rail, looking out over the glittering ocean to the blimp's right, where they could see a large island not too far off ahead.

The girl leaned on the rail, lifting herself up on her tippy-toes. She relaxed and glanced up at Robin, and then at Valerie.

"It's not… some evil curse?"

Valerie crunched her nose and asked, "What?"

"This werewolf stuff… When we found out mom had dealt with it, I thought I was supposed to hate her. I even did." She lowered herself so that her face was resting on her folded hands on the railing. "Then Allen was bitten, sealing the deal, and… she was dead. I couldn't hate her anymore, and realized I was a horrible person for ever having those thoughts to begin with. The doubts never went away, though."

Valerie stared at her, uneasy with this comforting role. Finally she put a hand on the young girl's shoulder. "There's nothing evil about it, and I'm sure your mom forgives you, wherever she is."

"But you think she's out there still, somewhere?" The girl perked up, hopeful. "My dad says so."

"I honestly have no idea," Valerie replied. "But if it helps you sleep, then I say believe whatever you want to believe. It's not like believing one way or another will hurt you, right? When you're dead, it's either true or not, and nothing else matters."

The girl smiled. "My name's Em."

"We're—"

"Valerie and Robin," Em said. "Yeah, I know. My brother, Allen, is the werewolf. The other one, Leo, is always looking out for us, even though I'm older than him."

"Sometimes the most powerful ones need the most looking after," Robin said, her voice dry through her mask.

"Who'll tell them?" Bronson asked, and they turned to see him walking out to the railing. He smiled at his daughter and then said. "Someone needs to land that blimp, and I have a feeling they don't know how."

"She does?" Valerie asked.

"Yes, I do," Em said. "But… I don't really want to be the one to interrupt whatever's going on over there."

"As if you don't know," Robin said with a scoff.

"When we're around my dad, I don't," Em said with a wink.

"Okay, okay," Bronson said. "Covering my ears."

"It's okay, I'll go over there with Em," Valerie offered. "That way… we're sure you won't sell us out or otherwise betray us."

Em frowned in confusion. "What? How so?"

"She means you'll be like a hostage," Robin said, bluntly, earning a red flush in Bronson's cheeks.

"No," Valerie said, "we know each other too well for that, right?"

Bronson nodded. "We're bonded. There'd be no need."

"Exactly."

Em just shook her head, lost in all this, and said, "Whatever. Let's get in there and stop those two from fucking—er, I mean, whatever they're doing."

Bronson just shook his head and walked off. "I'll be landing and working to get some images out of my head. When it's time, follow my lead."

"You sure you've got this?" Valerie asked Em.

The girl smiled and nodded, but looked out at the ship. "Um, how are we getting over there, exactly?"

"Ever played that 'swing me' game, where your parents would swing you by the arms?"

"You can't be serious," the girl said, going visibly pale. "I'll break my legs when I land."

"Trust us," Robin said, and then together they took her arms, and swung her, releasing her into the air so that she went flying into the other blimp.

"See you over there," Valerie said, and then she ran to the edge and pushed off with a thrust, so that while Em went up in an arc, Valerie almost went straight. She landed on the other deck with a roll, stopped herself with a kick against the deck that put a dent in the wood, and then held out her arms to catch Em.

"DON'T EVER DO THAT TO ME AGAIN!" Em screamed, but when Valerie set her down, she started laughing.

Robin landed at the railing with a thud, held on, and then pulled herself over the side to join them. "What's up with laughie-the-clown?"

"That was... fun," Em said between laughs. "Holy shit."

"Something tells me you aren't the good girl your dad probably wishes you were," Valerie said, chuckling.

"No, but I don't think he really cares." Em wiped a tear from her eye and stopped laughing finally. "Goody-gals don't stand as much of a chance of surviving these days."

"True enough," Robin said. "So... who gets the job?"

"I'll do it," Em said.

"Thought you didn't want to... Oh, an act in front of your dad?"

Em just shrugged.

"Do it," Robin said, and Valerie could tell by her voice that she was smiling under that mask.

"Robin!" Valerie shook her head.

"It'll be funny, and the girl's probably never seen a grown man's... you know."

Valerie was about to protest further, but then she just laughed and motioned toward the door. "Whatever."

Em cleared her throat, adjusted the buttoned-down vest she wore under her purple jacket—one very similar to the one Valerie had found on her trip over to America—and then made for the door.

"This is wrong," Valerie said to Robin.

"So wrong," Robin replied with a chuckle. "I like this look on you, by the way."

Valerie glanced down at her pirate outfit, then at the violet dress Robin had on, and smiled. "You too, though, probably better when we can get that mask off of you."

A moment of silence followed, until they heard a yelp, Royland shouting, "Get out!" and Cammie laughing.

Em came running out, her eyes wide, and she mouthed, "Holy shit," just before a totally nude Cammie came running out after her.

"What gives?" Cammie asked, seeing Valerie and Robin.

"We're there. Put on your clothes," Valerie replied.

Cammie pointed at Em, mouth open as if she was going to say something, and then just chuckled.

"Whatever," she said as she went back inside.

For a minute, nobody said a thing, and then Robin and Valerie started cracking up.

"So?" Valerie finally asked.

Em just nodded, eyes still wide, and then said, "Cammie's a lucky gal. Damn lucky."

They all laughed again, and then went inside to get ready to land the blimp.

CHAPTER NINE

Isle of the Prince

The island seemed to grow larger as the blimps drifted in their descent, and Valerie was reminded of her first time arriving in Old Manhattan. She had just found out about people there hunting vampires for blood, so had been quite uneasy about the whole situation.

Here it was slightly different, in that now she knew her powers and knew that nobody stood a chance against her. Otherwise, it was the same, though—she was riding into the open mouth of a sleeping dragon.

Sure, she was practically unstoppable, but the people around her weren't. The people she cared about could easily be hurt or killed if she got careless or was simply looking the other way. The anxiety was still present, even if she hid it behind a wall of confidence.

The sound of music carried up from the town. Valerie was glad to see the orange hue setting across the city, and when she looked up to the blowing wind, she paused to stare at the endless stretches of land bathed in orange, blanketed by thick, red and yellow clouds. The bright spot of sun shone through faintly, hovering at the edge of the horizon.

A man below was waving his arms and pointing to a field, where the other blimp was already landing.

"Better hold onto something," Em shouted from the control center.

Valerie scoffed, but then thought better of trying to look tough. The last thing she needed was for her first act as a pirate to be flopping around on a blimp or even going over the side. Great strength and speed didn't always mean perfect balance, though they did help.

Cammie joined her, while Royland and Robin stayed inside. The two of them held onto the railing and watched the shadow as it grew larger, and then they landed with a jolt.

"We have to take out this whole place," Cammie said. "You realize that, don't you? If Old Manhattan is going to survive, we can't allow this piracy to continue."

"New York," Valerie said. "We're calling it that again. But... take it slow. We need information on them first. They have other camps, and a headquarters out west."

"West is land... why are pirates based inland?"

Valerie gestured to the blimp they were in. "It's not like ships are limited to the sea."

"True... and I guess they could be better defended away from the water."

Then a man jogged over, but Bronson intercepted him along the way and, while they were shouting at each other, Valerie and Cammie walked back into the control room to find Robin there, smirking.

"What?" Valerie asked, then saw where she nodded to. Em was leaning back, her eyes on Royland's crotch.

Cammie laughed. "Didn't get enough of a view earlier?"

Em looked up, her cheeks went bright red, and she made a bee-line for the door.

"You ladies are mean," Royland said, adjusting his pants in a self-conscious kind of way.

"She's tough, she'll get over it," Cammie said.

"I'm not talking about her." He stared pointedly at Valerie's breasts. "Do you like that?"

She smiled. "I do, actually, but I think Cammie here's about to kick your ass."

"We get the point," Cammie said. "We'll stop objectifying your huge c—"

"Come on," he interrupted. "Do they need to know everything about us?"

"You're so old fashioned," Cammie said, going to him and wrapping her arms around his neck. "That's what I love about you."

His eyes went wide, but she pulled back. "Wait, no, I said 'love about you,' I didn't say 'that's why I love you' or whatever is going on in your head."

He narrowed his eyes, as if unsure.

"You all heard me," Cammie said, turning to Valerie and Robin. "Right?"

"Hmm, sounded like you said you love him to me," Robin said with a grin.

Valerie laughed, playing along. "This is all so romantic. Maybe the pirates have a bottle of wine to toast this momentous occasion."

"Oh, come on!" She threw her hands up and said, "Everyone, chill. Just... this isn't funny."

"You don't like it when it's directed at you, huh?" Royland chuckled.

"Having a donkey dong and being accused of saying something you didn't say are two very different things."

Valerie held up a hand. "Yeah, but neither of those things are necessarily bad. Might want to keep that in mind."

"Unless it hurts," Robin said, looking back at Royland's crotch again.

He covered it and made an annoyed grunt, heading for the door, but then stopped. "Dammit, I can't go outside yet. Remind me never to travel with you three ladies together after this."

"He has a point," Valerie said, looking down at her breasts, which had not only grown when Michael had given her extra power, but were now pressed up tight, thanks to her pirate dress. She never understood why they had grown, but had to assume that the nanocytes or whatever it was he had told her were in her blood upgraded her in other ways than just for combat—like reproductive purposes. Or maybe it was an accidental side effect.

When she looked up, everyone was staring at her breasts, too. Yeah, that felt really awkward.

"No more objectifying anyone here, got it?" She looked pointedly at Cammie, then Robin. "We need to be a team, and that means trusting each other. Not holding resentment."

"He's a guy," Cammie said in response. "What guy doesn't want this kind of objectification?"

Valerie turned to Royland for an answer.

He pursed his lips, thinking about it. "Good point, but still... I don't know, it just feels weird, everyone here imagining me nude. There's definitely a good side to that, you could say, but at the same time, I guess it makes me uncomfortable on some unexplainable level."

"Sexual tension," Cammie replied.

"What?"

"If we all just stripped down and got it out of the way, you know, out of our system, it wouldn't be awkward, and we could all move on."

Everyone stared at her now, but she just smiled back.

"We're not doing that," Valerie said. "And Cammie, I think you need help."

"Help… in a sexual way?" She took Royland's hand. "Nope, got that covered."

"I was thinking more in an it's weird to be okay sharing your man kind of way."

"As odd as this sounds from me," Royland said, kissing her hand. "I agree. I mean, maybe it'd be nice if you were a little jealous about the idea of me with another woman."

"I would be if I wasn't there, too," Cammie said, as if that made all the sense in the world.

Valerie hung her head in frustration.

"Um, guys?" Robin was at the doorway, no mask on, smiling. "In case you didn't notice, all this talking lasted long enough for the sun to set. It's pirate city time."

"Wonderful!" Royland said, and Valerie was just as happy to have a reason to move on from the awkward conversation.

They all climbed down from the blimp to find Bronson slipping some coins into the stranger's hand. With a smile, the stranger nodded their way and walked off.

"Bastard says it's for protection," Bronson said when they had joined him.

"As if we need protection," Cammie scoffed.

"Maybe we don't," Bronson replied, "but the blimps do. A couple shots into those balloons and we'd be grounded."

"You have somewhere to stay until we need to get out of here?" Valerie asked him, glancing over his shoulder at his three kids who were just walking over to join them.

"I've made some contacts," he said. "We'll be safe."

"You have a plan?" Robin asked Valerie.

Cammie interjected, "Kill 'em all. Let God sort 'em out."

"The fuck kind of saying is that?" Bronson asked.

"Dad, mouth," Allen said. The kids were at his side now.

"Sorry, son." Bronson shook his head, then looked at Valerie, nervously. "Please tell me you have a plan."

Valerie laughed at the pout on Cammie's face, then said,

"While we might eventually find that killing ends up being a necessity, I agree with what I think the Captain's getting at. What're we here for? To stop them from pirating, so that New York—and the rest of the world, really—can prosper."

"So… we have to kill them all." Cammie said, folding her arms across her chest.

"Or we have to take control," Valerie said with a smile.

Bronson frowned. "It's… impossible." His frown gave way to a smile. "But I like the way you think."

"Thinking has nothing to do with it," Royland said with a laugh. "Why would we even want to keep them alive? These are cutthroats, thieves, and, er…" he glanced at the kids, then finished with, "…worse."

"Every last one of 'em," Cammie added with a disdainful glance at the pirate city.

"Is that so?" Bronson asked, holding his youngest son close. "Until just a while ago, I was one of them, in a way. Lots of people are, because they aren't given a choice or simply see no alternative."

"These are pirates we're talking about here," Royland said. "Just because you fell in with them, doesn't mean we should take it easy here."

"I'm not saying we should take it easy." Bronson stood his ground, not backing down from the vampire in front of him, and Valerie had to respect that. "But I'm saying we separate the rotten ones from the rest. You don't think there's people out there right now who think all vampires are bad? Who'd take to the streets and burn every last one of you alive, simply because of stories they've heard? Of your reputation?" He scoffed, glaring at Royland. "There're some among you who I'm sure deserve this, but others less so."

"Fuck. You."

"You don't think I've heard about you?" He looked at the rest of the group. "Did he tell you all the truth of his past? I've heard stories up here. Royland the Merciless, that's you, right?"

Royland backhanded Bronson, knocking him to the ground. Immediately his boy, Allen, had transformed and was attacking Royland. The boy actually held his ground fairly well, but Valerie stepped in and pulled them apart.

"Learn your place, boy," Royland said, then froze as everyone stared at him. "I—I had to lead my clan back then! Choices were made, none that I wouldn't give up in a second if I had that as an option. But I don't. I have to live with my choices, and do my best to make amends for them."

Bronson stood and held a hand out for his boy to relax, then smiled. "Point proven."

"Excuse me?"

"Point proven," he repeated. "There are men, women, and yes, even children in there who have done some bad stuff, and walked away rich. We can bet on that. But there are many who would give it all up in a second if they knew there was another lifestyle waiting for them. If they knew there was a leader who could take them away from this pirate life."

He turned to Valerie, waiting, but to her surprise, Cammie was the one who spoke up.

"He's right," she said. "And I'll be the one to lead them. Well, not just me…" She took Royland's hand and held it to her chest, clutched in both of hers. "Both of us. Because none of your past matters to me, none of that shit. And we have to show the world that there's a chance for redemption. If there isn't, we're all doomed."

Royland's gaze remained firm, but he nodded. "If they don't try to kill us, they can live. I'll stand by such a rule."

"Those who want to can move to New York, but only if we feel they're trustworthy. If they stay here, they fall under us and our new rule."

"Well then, let's go bag ourselves some pirates, shall we?"

Bronson said with a shrug. He pointed to the pirate city, diverting the group's attention. They were at the outskirts of it, but farther in they could just make out the sound of cheering and music and the warm glow of large fires.

"That's where we'll want to be," Bronson said, and they all stared at the spot down by the shore.

Fires roared around a well-preserved building from the old days, tall glass windows and a colorful wave of decorative architecture running along the front. A tall building stood behind it, and two incoming blimps could be seen passing overhead. The building might have once been a hotel, but Valerie guessed now was the housing base for the most respected pirates on the island. Crowds were gathered there, small dots moving about in the distance, but it was clear this was the spot to be.

"Many islands weren't hurt as bad during the aftermath to the Great Collapse," Bronson said, as if reading her mind. "This one included. Yes, vegetation and whatnot suffered, but the crazies were kept at bay, and the people here were able to last, even had a ship—a regular sail boat—that they managed to get afloat... the days that followed led to intercepting a blimp at port, and, eventually, what you see before you."

"We look the part?" Valerie asked, glancing down at her pressed up cleavage and cringing.

He nodded. "Some of the pirates have been experimenting with various tech, like what you saw back there with those metal gloves. Most of it is trigger-based—they make connection, darts shoot out, for example. But I've seen a weird device on a pirate's back with steam coming out of it, others with strange additions to their swords. Just... be careful."

"You take care of those three kids. We can take care of ourselves."

"Down south, they hunted vampire blood," Bronson said. "Well, up here they hunt vampires and Weres, but not for blood—it's for sport. The UnknownWorld did less of a good job keeping itself unknown around these parts, so now it's the ultimate sign of success if you can mount a head on your wall.

"A human head?" Robin asked, horrified.

"That's the problem, isn't it? You can't really tell if it's human or Were once it's on the wall."

"We are human," Valerie corrected him. "Just modified."

He nodded, forcing a smile as he looked at his Were boy. "I know that, you know that, but I'm afraid they don't know that yet." With a gesture to the incoming blimps, he said, "We best be moving on, unless we want to start here."

"If we want answers," Robin said, staring off into the distance and the fires that lit up the night sky, "who're we looking for?"

"The prince, of course," Bronson replied. "When you see him, you'll know."

"We'll escort you to the safe house," Valerie said. "Then you and your family stay safe, we'll break off and look for him."

"And if we find him?" Royland asked.

"We need information on slaving operations in these parts," Valerie replied. "We might need him to leverage bigger fish, and, at some point, we'll need him out of the picture so that we can move in and fix this place."

"Alive then," Cammie said. "Alive pirates are my least favorite kind."

"Then you might want to avoid looking in a mirror," Valerie said with a chuckle.

Cammie adjusted the black button-up coat and adjusted her black, felt hat. "I love the hat, though," she admitted. "It'll do well enough to replace my old one." She pulled one of the swords she'd taken from the fallen pirates, not so different from her old kali-sticks, except that these blades weren't hidden within wood. "And these will do fine."

Valerie, too, had picked up a belt with two blades attached, though hers were longer and thinner. Not your typical cutlass, used as much for the force of the strike as the blade itself. Hers, she guessed, as she didn't know much about pirate blades, were more like modified rapiers. After a quick test and a smile to reassure the others, Valerie nodded and said, "We all know our mission, let's get to it."

With that, they began their march into the pirate city to begin their hunt for the pirate prince. Valerie thought it funny that some had once called her the vampire princess, and now here she was, seeking out a prince. Only, in this fairy tale, she was damn sure it wouldn't end with him winning her hand. Instead, she would tear out his heart.

CHAPTER TEN

Old Manhattan

Sandra had slept most of the afternoon and woke to find that it was dark outside.

"Diego?" she called out, and glanced around, waiting for a response. When none came, she turned on the bedside lamp and walked into the dining room.

Again she called out for him, but no answer came. She turned on the main light and cringed as it flickered, too. Just another reminder that they hadn't perfected this city yet. One day, she swore to herself, they would have this whole place operating like the old days—better even.

She meandered over to the cupboard and found some crackers to munch on, poured a glass of water, and then went to the window. Outside, a police pod passed by, dark blue silhouette in the night with red lights trailing. A yellow glow rose up out of the city, and she wondered what all of the people out there were doing. Not sleeping yet, apparently. Many were likely just getting off of work and making their way to the food stalls along Capital Square, where they could find bowls of noodles, fried rice, and at one cart, even hot dogs.

The thought made her mouth water, so she jammed another cracker in there and chased it with a swig of water.

Where was Diego? She turned to see if the bathroom light was on, starting to feel the tightness in her chest that only came with worry, and then paused. There on the table was a piece of parchment. A note!

She darted over and picked it up.

The note read: Sorry, love, didn't want to wake you. Donnoly called a meeting at Enforcer HQ.

Sandra stared at the note for a moment, then noticed she was clenching her hand hard enough for her fingernails to hurt her palms. What the hell? They were having meetings without her now.

Maybe that shouldn't have bothered her, but it did. She had helped take control in the days following the departure of Commander Strake and the CEOs. She'd moved into leadership positions more than once, when others weren't around to do so.

Then again, she was the one who wanted to keep life more simple, to start the café and focus on sweets and wine. There wasn't any reason to complain, so why did she want to kick something?

She smiled, remembering one reason her emotions might be going crazy right now, and rubbed her belly. A little baby was growing in there, and that might mean some emotional shifts from time to time.

Still, that didn't mean she had to sit here and let them leave her out of whatever the hell was happening. Throwing on a light jacket over her T-shirt and changing into a pair of jeans, she finished her water and went for the door, then had to double back when she remembered how being pregnant meant using the bathroom way more than normal. She didn't want to be halfway there and have to pop a squat in some alley—not without her Were boyfriend, or husband... nearby to protect her.

When she was done, she made her way over to Enforcer HQ

without incident and was soon riding the elevators to Colonel Donnoly's office. That was where most of the meetings took place, so she figured the same would be true this night.

Indeed, a low hum of chatter emerged from the office as she stepped out of the elevator. When she threw open the office doors, everyone turned to look at her. Donnoly sat at the head of the table, Esmerelda and Presley nearby, and Diego at the opposite end of the table.

"Honey, you're awake!" Diego stood and pulled out the chair next to him.

She glared and sat, then asked, "Why was I excluded?"

Donnoly pursed his lips and motioned to her belly. "We just assumed…"

"No, don't assume. Until I'm laid back with a baby coming out of me, I'm still in commission." A couple in the room cringed at that image. "Seriously? We've all killed, and you have problems with the idea of life being brought into the world?" Donnoly laughed, but Sandra glared at him. "You tried to exclude me based on this. You aren't getting off so easily."

"They're just looking out for you," Esmerelda said, coldly.

"Let me look out for myself." For a moment she considered asking what the hell Esmerelda was doing here anyway, but from seeing the way the woman had acted toward Donnoly earlier, she didn't have any doubts.

And then the awkward silence came… and dragged on. And on.

Finally Sandra cleared her throat, leaned forward with her palms on the table, and said, "Get on with it then."

"Several matters were on the table," Donnoly said. "One of them being your new friend."

"He's good to go."

Donnoly arched an eyebrow, but nodded. "Which brings us to the second item, and a perfect opportunity to test him out."

"I vouch for him," Sandra said, growing exasperated. "There's no need."

"No offense," Donnoly said, slowly looking around the room. "Most of you haven't been part of this city longer than a couple months. As much as I trust you all—"

"Are you shitting me?" Sandra stood now, anger flaring. "After all we've been through?"

"Honey," Diego said, standing and taking her arm. "The baby…"

She pulled her arm free, rolling her eyes at the fact that he would use that now. "What's this test then?"

Donnoly had the gall to look to Diego before saying, "There's talk of a group outside the city walls. Possibly made up of some old faction members, maybe an escaped leader. Talk is, they're going to make a move on the city. Try to attack from within. They know these tunnels better than most of us, to be frank. We have to hit them before they make their move."

Sandra sat back down with a sigh. "When's all this going to be over?"

"When we're all working together," a voice said from the doorway and they turned to see Sergeant Garcia. "Until you all and the FDG are working hand in hand, these lands won't be safe."

Others looked to Donnoly, but he said, "Garcia here will be tested, but not in a 'we don't trust him' sort of way. More of a 'we shouldn't trust anyone, but he seems legit' way."

Garcia chuckled. "Fair enough."

"Didn't the Black Plague group of vampires exist not too far from where the FDG is located?"

"A small army of vampire assassins?" Garcia laughed out loud. "The FDG is equipped well, but not well enough to handle that, or not when they're keeping hidden, anyway. TH is smart, he sees the value in partnering with you all—a bunch of vampires and Weres, along with smart leaders."

"Smart enough to somewhat trust you, anyway," Donnoly said. "Is that it?"

Garcia nodded. "Seems like a qualification of intelligence if ever I heard one."

Sandra hated this—she'd always hated watching Valerie run off to the fight, but at least then she was worried about a vampire with crazy strength and healing power. Sure, Diego was a Were and could heal, too, but he wasn't on the same level as Valerie.

She turned to him, eyes full of concern, but he already seemed to know what she was thinking.

"I'll be careful," he whispered.

"You want me to watch over him?" Garcia said with a broad smile.

"Ha!" Diego said in a fake laugh. "Say that again when I'm keeping those nut-jobs off of you. We'll see."

"Do they really even stand a chance of leading an attack on the city?" Esmerelda asked. "I mean, is this something we should bother ourselves with to the degree that we're having night meetings about it?"

Everyone turned to Donnoly, who seemed to think about it but, Sandra surmised, had already considered all angles of this topic.

"Even so," he said, "we want the people of New York to know they're safe, that they don't have to worry about being invaded. Sure, this time it might be small, but fear of the unknown can eat away at the best of us."

"Hit 'em strong and hard, and never let the citizens know a threat existed in the first place," Garcia said, nodding his approval. "I like the way you people think. Smart."

"It's settled then." Donnoly stood, and others followed suit. "Get some rest. We'll take a small group of Weres and vampires out in the early morning, well before sunrise."

Sandra lingered behind with Diego, watching Garcia and Donnoly meander off, deep in conversation.

"Less than a full day here," she noted. "Moving fast."

"That's his job, isn't it?" Diego asked.

"Yeah, sure." Sandra was about to stand, when she saw a look cross Diego's face. "What is it?"

"Just something I heard from Bradley, that large Were from the Golden City. About some of the Weres being uneasy."

"That's nothing new," she said. "Weres working and training alongside vampires… seems like nothing to me, but it's not like there haven't been issues there."

"Like a human and a Were, kinda?" He chuckled. "Just because something's had problems in the past doesn't mean it should be discarded."

She took his hand, lovingly. "Of course."

He shook his head. "You're missing the point."

"And that is?"

"That there might be more going on than a little unrest. He thinks we might end up with another group causing trouble from within."

"A mutiny?" She licked her lips, considering it. "Or does that word only apply to ships?"

"Regardless, you stay vigilant in the city. I'll do the worrying about the team on the road."

"I don't like it," she said.

He squeezed her hand and forced a smile. "You don't have to."

CHAPTER ELEVEN

Isle of the Prince

Valerie and her group stayed to the shadows as they made their way into the closest part of the city, not far from their destination.

"You sure you'll be safe here?" she asked Bronson as he herded his children up a staircase between two buildings.

"Safe in a place like this?" he scoffed. "No one's safe in a place like this. Well, maybe you, but no normal person. That said, I've learned to hold my own, and I have Allen here."

Allen paused in the doorway at the top of the stairs long enough to turn and show the yellow of his eyes, then disappeared within.

"I would say it's crazy to rely on a kid his age," Cammie said, "but if he's anything like I was, you'll be fine."

He nodded, paused, and held out his hand to Valerie.

"The hell's that?" she asked.

"In case I never see you again."

"You never see her again," Cammie interjected, "you're going to wish you'd asked for a lot more than a handshake."

Valerie rolled her eyes, but was glad to see her comment

made the man smile. Instead of the handshake she went in for a hug, conscious of her breasts pressed against him and wondering what guys thought of that—it wasn't like she did it on purpose, or not this time, anyway, but would guys realize that? Not likely.

"Just be safe," she said. "I'll need you on that blimp when it's time to move out."

He nodded, then headed up the stairs and out of sight.

"We need a guard here?" Robin asked.

Valerie thought about it, then shook her head. "He's survived this far. And having Allen with him improves his chance, so there you go."

Robin nodded, but glanced up to where the curtains moved at the window above. Probably one of the boys looking out. "I still don't feel right about leaving children here... not in a place like this."

"They're teens," Cammie reminded her. "And kinda badass teens, based on what they went through."

"And those children?" Valerie said, watching two boys run across the street, chasing some sort of rat or something. "They don't deserve to live like this. Who knows what we're facing here, or what horrors arise when we fail to take action."

Royland nodded, then Cammie. Finally, Robin said, "Let's liberate."

They walked toward the lights, Valerie in the lead. Every time a pirate passed, she expected to have to end a life. The pirates were either too drunk or just assumed she and her group were pirates as well, because they just walked on past, some pausing to drunkenly tip a hat.

Shouting came from ahead and, as they entered a path surrounded by shanties, the sound of more yelling came, then something snapping and the groans of man on man fighting.

"Remember," Valerie said with a glance back at Cammie's hands gripping her sword hilts, "we're not here for violence, yet."

"You sure about that?" Cammie said with a nod to one of the buildings ahead on the left.

Valerie squinted, wondering what Cammie was seeing, then saw the silhouette of a head—what she had at first assumed to be just another person, this one on a roof, was a head on a spike.

"Oh, for fuck's sake," Valerie said, feeling a bit queasy. It wasn't just a head, it was a woman's head.

They stepped out in a circular clearing, where a crowd was gathered to watch three men kicking and beating a fourth.

At a glance from Robin, Valerie held up a hand and turned to an old, balding man at her side.

"What'd he do?"

The man glanced at her, sneered in a way that showed off his black teeth, and said, "You ain't heard? That's his wife up there." The man gestured to the head on display. "Found out she was one of them, you know."

"One of…?"

"A werewolf. Dumb bastard insists she wasn't, but where's that gonna get him other than a shallow grave?"

Valerie sighed, not wanting to be part of this, but really seeing no choice. She gave Robin a nod, and Cammie grinned at her side.

"So much for staying low key," Valerie said as she followed Robin, who was pushing her way through the crowd. If there was one thing that girl hated, it was injustice and bullying. This was a whole lot of both.

"All right, everyone, time to—" Valerie started, but a thud sounded, interrupting her, and a second later one of the attackers collapsed from one of Robin's punches. Cammie was there at her side, kicking another's knee out before backhanding him so that he fell to the ground, unconscious.

"Real nice," Valerie said, rolling her eyes. She'd hoped they could try to keep some sense of secrecy here, but knocking a man unconscious with a backhand wasn't the best way toward that goal.

"You with him then?" the third attacker asked, then turned and spat on the bloodied man at his feet.

Not bothering to respond, Royland stepped forward and helped the bloodied man to stand while Valerie stepped forward to address the crowd.

"Show's over," she said. "As is the hunt for our kind. Attack one of us again, and you'll all answer for your crime."

"Who the fuck do you think you are, walking in here and—" the man stopped talking and started screaming instead as Cammie grabbed him by the balls and lifted him into the air with one hand. "Fuck-fuck-fuck!"

She released her hold and he fell to the ground, howling in pain. A quick kick shut him up, though he spat blood and stared at her with piercing blue eyes.

"Did these men kill his wife?" Valerie asked, addressing the crowd.

"She was a werewolf," one of them shouted.

"A creature of the dammed!" came the shrill voice of another.

A tall man in a long black coat stepped forward, dreadlocks hanging over his shoulders. He smiled and said, "She got what she deserved."

Valerie stared at this man and took a sniff. Nope, just normal human. She smiled back, and then pushed out with fear, causing everyone in the crowd to either step back or cower.

"She's a witch!" the man shouted, regaining his composure faster than the rest. "You saw what she did, put her head up there with the werewolf."

"A...?" Valerie guffawed, caught off guard with that one.

"Oh, I'd love to see this," Royland said, motioning the guy forward. "Don't suppose anyone has any popcorn? No? Yeah, you're right, I'd hate to get blood and guts confused with the butter."

"What's wrong with your friend?" a short woman asked Valerie with a nod in Royland's direction.

"He's got a thing for idiots getting their comeuppance," Valerie replied. "We all do."

"Can I just cut him in half?" Cammie asked, glaring. "Skip the show and go right to dessert?"

"Screw that," Valerie replied. "I say we teach him a lesson and let him run back to his prince to tell him all about it."

The crowd hushed at the mention of their prince, many still terrified from the fear Valerie had pushed onto them. Oddly, she noted, this tall man's aura seemed calm.

"I don't think he'll be the only one learning this lesson," she said, ears perking at the sound of something behind them. A great whirring came as a man with a chainsaw came at her. She dodged left, only to find the man with dreadlocks pulling out two sabers and swinging her way.

Dodging these wasn't much of a challenge, but when another opened fire with an old AK-47 that hit three innocents, one of them a young teen, she got pissed. The AK-47 was in her hands before she knew it, and it was slamming over and over into the large man's face until he fell back to the ground, twitched, and stopped moving.

The crowd fell back, no one else attacking, except for the two with the chainsaw and the one with long dreadlocks.

Wait, no... the chainsaw fell to the ground, the man's arm still attached to it, and the man fell the other way, blood spewing.

Cammie nodded from the other side of him, sword still held out.

"What's your name?" Valerie asked the dreadlock guy as she approached, AK-47 held up like a street-thug. She hadn't wanted it to happen like this, but she kicked herself for that thought. These were street thugs, after all, playing pirate.

When he didn't respond, she laughed and shot a round into

his foot—or meant to, but the weapon gave out a burst of rounds that ripped into his leg.

He collapsed to the ground, grunting in pain, teeth clenched to avoid yelling out.

"What is his name?" she repeated, this time to the crowd.

"Captain—Captain Bairne," a teen boy said, stepping forward. He was shirtless except for an open vest—a look that never would have worked here before the warming effects of the World's Worst Day Ever.

"River, the Prince'll kill ya!" a woman behind him said, trying to pull him back. He pulled himself free, pointing to the teen who'd been shot, but was no longer moving. "Fuck Bairne, and fuck the Prince," he shouted for all to hear. "Oliver's dead because of those pricks." He took two long strides and stomped down on the bloodied leg of Captain Bairne, but the man was still about his senses enough to lunge for River.

Royland was too quick for that, though, and was pulling the two apart within a second. He tossed Bairne to the crowd, a couple of whom helped him stand.

"Well, then…" Valerie smiled at them, showing her vampire teeth. "Tell your Prince that I'm here, and willing to talk." She raised her voice, turning to address the crowd. "Anyone here who wishes to live may do so with my permission. I'm not here to enslave you, but to set you free. You want treasure… you need treasure, it's clear from your hollow cheeks and ravenous eyes. Well, I can give it to you, in terms of work. I can keep you safe, keep you away from having to steal from others."

"Bullshit," a woman in a wide pirate's hat said. She tilted her head to the side, her black hair tucked behind her ears. "How the 'ell you gonna do all that?"

"We've taken Old Manhattan," Valerie said. "The CEOs are gone, Strake is gone, and—"

"No fucking way," the woman said, suddenly standing

straight, looking at Valerie and the dead and injured, then taking a step back. "You're really her, ain't ya?"

"Her?"

"The devil walking," the woman said in almost a whisper, then cleared her throat. "The vampire princess. The one they say took 'em all out with her fangs and claws."

Valerie licked her lips, glancing about. She wasn't using her fear at all, but faces were pale, eyes wide, mouths open. Even Bairne and his men were staring in silence.

"We liberated that city," Valerie said. "Saved humans, both modified and not, and have set about rebuilding it into the New York it once was—a city of awe and wonder. The happiest place on earth, I've heard."

"You slaughtered men and women!" Bairne said, laughing. "I've heard the stories, we all have!"

"Some of those were our brothers and sisters in arms," one of the women next to him said, and she held up a stump. "This was a present from one of yours, a fucking werewolf. Now we hunt your kind and theirs. But looks like the hunt's over, eh? Grand fucking prize turkey just flew up to our doorstep."

"You have it all wrong," Valerie said. "Well, maybe not you, because it sounds like you were one of Strake's Enforcers..." When the woman didn't respond, Valerie nodded and addressed the crowd. "I hear you're all pirates, but I bring you a shot at redemption. This is what New York is all about now—new beginnings. Yes, even you, lady with one arm and a crappy attitude, you would be welcome in New York."

"We'd make a deal with the devil, and be foolish enough to leave everything behind based on that deal?" another man from the audience shouted, but his voice carried with it a sense of hope.

"I am no devil," Valerie said. "I am here to ensure justice is carried out at all levels, to see that my kind, vampires and Weres, are treated as equals to non-modified humans. And to assist any who will accept my help."

"Well then, you can go to hell," Bairne said, and turned to hobble away, his followers close at his heels.

"I expect to hear from this prince character very soon." Valerie called after them.

"Trust me, you will," Bairne called out as he disappeared around the bend.

Valerie turned to the crowd again, waiting, and then said, "You all have a choice to make. But you can wait until I've dealt with the Prince before you make up your damn minds."

Then she turned and motioned for her team to gather close, and waited, staring at the boy they'd called River. He looked hesitantly her way, then walked over and waited.

"Do you want to be part of what we're doing here?" Valerie asked.

"He's just a kid," Royland interjected.

River's eyes shot over to Royland, fierce, but he was smart enough to keep his mouth shut. Valerie could respect that.

"Answer the question," Robin said to the boy.

"I ain't serving the prince no more," he said. "Too many lives are just thrown away up here, too much power given to jackholes simply because they dish out the most violence. You run this New York place like that?"

Valerie shook her head.

"Well, then you got yourself a new recruit."

Robin rolled her eyes and said, "Yay," then turned back to watch the dispersing crowd going about their business. Several had stayed, but not more than a handful.

"They're mostly too scared," River said. "And they should be. This guy, he's not normal. He's basically established himself as a god up here. Calls himself the Prince and goes between here and out west, carrying goods to—"

"West?" Robin asked, suddenly interested. "Did you ever go?

Do you, I mean… do you know anything about the slavers out there?"

Valerie frowned. Real slick.

"Nothing," River said. "Sorry, but I ain't traveled that way. Most I've done was find my way here, just me and my aunt there."

He nodded to the woman who had pulled him back earlier, now hovering with the few other leftovers.

She seemed to have taken this as her cue, because she stepped forward and said, "We shouldn't be doing this. I told you we shouldn't have come here in the first place, and now you want to turn your back on these murderers, basically declare war on the worst of them?"

"This Prince character?" River scoffed, then turned to Valerie. "It's a stupid title. Rumor is he used to fight alongside some great warriors, true survivalists, but he's the only one of them left. Leaves it open for anyone to challenge him and, if they win, he would hand over leadership. Problem is, the handful of men who've tried were taken down in one or two punches, like swatting flies. Fucker's only been here a couple months and already has everyone licking out of his milk bowl."

"Licking out of his…?" Cammie laughed. "I don't think I've heard that one before. I'm stealing it."

He nodded to her and seemed about to wink, when Royland caught his eye. Instead, he actually took a step back.

"Wait," Valerie said, deep in thought, "you said a couple of months?"

"Could be three or four," he replied. "Why?"

"Seems like only yesterday, but… it hasn't even been half a year yet since my brother tried to invade Old Manhattan."

"And you said some of his top dogs escaped," Royland nodded, catching on quick.

"Wait, you mean…?" River cocked his head. "He might be like you?"

Valerie nodded, then showed her extended fangs. The boy looked like he was about to wet himself, but stood his ground.

"He's never let on, if that's the case," River said.

The other pirates who had stayed behind gathered around now, whispering amongst themselves. Valerie decided it was time to make this official. She turned to the group, held up her hands for silence, and then said, "I am a vampire."

Everyone fell silent immediately.

"So is he," she said pointing to Royland, then Cammie, "and she's a werewolf. A Were. But it's not like the stories say, and it's time that became common knowledge. We can't keep the UnkownWorld unknown forever. The truth is…" She looked at their lost, beaten, but hopeful faces, and sighed. "The truth is, we are modified humans, that's all. There's something in our blood that helped us change, something that's not evil in any way. In fact, and now you're going to have to keep up with me here, the point of these changes was to help establish earth's defense in the war of all wars."

"The days of big war are over," a man said from the small crowd. "Civilization has fallen."

"This isn't a war of earth," she said. "Rather, for earth."

"Aliens?" the man said, and then scoffed. "If this woman is for real, she's off her rocker."

"It's all true," she replied, "even the part about me being off my rocker, if that means bat-shit crazy. But I'm bat-shit crazy about one thing, and that's saving this world."

River's aunt scoffed. "So, you're like, what? One of those super heroes of the old days?"

"Super… whats?" Valerie asked, glancing around at her friends, who looked mostly as lost as her, all but Cammie.

"From old books, comics, no?" Cammie laughed. "Really? We had a couple that had survived the Great Collapse… mostly it's men and women in tights and capes, helping people in trouble."

Valerie glanced down at her pirate dress, and chuckled. "Not exactly your tights and cape, but sure, think of me, or us, as you will. We're just enhanced humans, trying to make a difference."

"And if we trust you," River's aunt went on, "how do we know this is the case? How do we know you won't simply wait until we're asleep and then suck our blood? Or her," she gestured to Cammie, "turn into a wolf on the full moon and attack us?"

Valerie shook her head. "That's not how it works, not remotely. Cammie?"

With one finger pointed at the quarter moon, Cammie let her teeth sharpen and her eyes glow yellow. She even allowed a bit of a snout to form, hair and all, before pulling it back.

"You see?" Valerie took a moment, letting it sink in. She sensed a heat coming from the crowd, from some piercing, untrusting, but from others it was warm, wanting to accept. "Not all of you, and that's fine."

"You can read our minds, too, then?"

"No, but I can sense emotions. Those of you who want to be part of this, to become superior heroes—"

"It's super heroes," Cammie corrected her.

"Whatever." Valerie turned to River's aunt and held out a hand. "You first. Are you with your nephew? Will you be one of us?"

The woman laughed, then frowned, looking at her hand, then shrugged as she shook. "What the hell. If River's getting mixed up in all this, it ain't like I'd be safe anyhow."

"Martha?" one of the men said. "We're here to survive, that's what we all agreed upon."

"And that's what I'm doing," Martha replied. "Me and my nephew are latching onto the biggest lion in the pack, you can join, too, or run off and hide."

"You all don't need to fight," Valerie said. "That's not what I'm demanding here, because, honestly, the four of us can fight just fine. What we want is people we know will stay out of our way, and be ready when the time comes. Yes, you might have to defend yourself when the other side stops holding their punches, when the situation gets dirty, but is that any different from now?"

"Different in some ways, not so much in others," the man replied. He looked from her to Martha, then nodded. The others seemed surprised by this, but none interrupted. "Best move out of here quick then, if you all don't want to just be mowed down by the Prince's followers."

"We've got nothing to worry about," Cammie said, hand on her hip. She tilted her hat forward so that the shadows covered her eyes.

"You might not, but anyone aligning with you ought to be off the streets. We have shelter nearby, where we can brief you on the island. Help you figure out your next move."

Valerie smiled, thinking how nice it was that they'd be discussing a thought-out plan. That didn't happen as often as she wished it did.

"She has a point," Royland said. "Until we know where their power structures lie, we don't want to be setting up our friends for failure."

"Or horrible deaths," Martha said.

"Or horrible death, if you want to put it more bluntly."

Valerie and Robin shared a look, and it was clear from Robin's furrowed brow and concerned look in her eyes that she agreed. They might actually have a chance to ask more of these people, about slaving operations out west and whatever else they could learn.

Cammie was looking at the fires by the large building on the shore not far off. She clearly wanted to run in, sword swinging and guns blazing, but she looked back to Valerie and waited.

"Lead the way," Valerie said. "Mr. ...?"

"Call me Leech," the man said, running a hand through his thinning hair. He had a thick beard that hung down to his chest, and wore a black shirt over brown pants with black shoes. He wasn't the flashy type like some of these so-called pirates, but had a sense of pride about him.

But that name.

"Leech?" she asked as they started walking.

He smiled as they ducked into the alley between some of the makeshift buildings, then followed a stream behind it. The moon glistened on the water, and the scent of fire-crisped meat carried with the wind.

"I'm not one of the main cutthroats or thieves around here," Leech said. "Some say it's my weakness. People like you might think it's a positive aspect of my person. Point is, I leech off of the rest of the pirates, but I've got me too many smarts for them to toss me out."

"Talks like an idiot sometimes," River interjected, "to make people think he's dumber than he really is, though."

Leech touched his nose and smiled. "On the nose. Always better to surprise them than the other way around."

They turned another bend and were just making their way up a slight hill when they heard what sounded like an explosion. Leech ducked, glancing back toward a large building that now had flames shooting out of it, and then they all saw the blimp lift into the air. It wasn't like the other blimps Valerie had seen so far. This one had cutting sails on the front and back, for quick turns, Valerie guessed. Metal lined the rails and, from this distance, it looked like an extra layer of thick canvas had been applied around the balloon itself. She could see that much because of her vampire sight, but not much else.

It was a war blimp.

And it was coming right for them. A rattling started, and then Leech was shouting for them to get down.

"Gatling gun!" River screamed out, and then the bullets began to rattle the ground around them.

CHAPTER TWELVE

Isle of the Prince

The blimp continued its trajectory, the Gatling gun interrupting the silence of night as red light appeared surrounded by smoke as bullets riddled the ground around Valerie and the others.

"Get below!" River said, snapping out of his stupor. He ran past and motioned for them to follow.

There was no time to hesitate. Sure, Valerie would likely recover from this, but she hated getting shot at all, let alone the feeling of hundreds of Gatling gun rounds all at once.

He led them to a point behind one of the huts, where he opened a hatch into a hole in the ground. Dirt sprayed up as more bullets hit, and someone cried out from nearby, although not one of their crew. They had all scattered, but now that the gun was turning to strafe the other side, they were reconvening and moving down into the hole, which turned out to be a tunnel.

"This happen often?" Robin shouted from behind.

"More than we're fucking comfortable with," Leech replied, climbing in behind them. "Anyone hit?"

Several replies of "nay" sounded, and Royland laughed before saying, "Sounds like a tunnel full of horses."

"Humor from Royland?" Cammie said, and Valerie realized those behind her had stopped. "Shit, you're hit aren't you?" She was pushing past the others, moving to get to him fast.

"We have to keep moving," River said, and Valerie gestured him to move on.

"Ain't the first time a vampire was shot," she said, realizing how odd it was to know someone was shot, but not worry in the least.

As they walked briskly along the tunnel, Valerie and her team continued introductions and gave River enough back-story to know about their recent excursion to Chicago.

"This man," River turned his head to look back in the near darkness, "he's basically started an army?"

"And you haven't heard the half of it," she replied. "They're going into space."

He just blinked.

"You know... space?" she asked.

"I'm familiar with the concept. But... you all can fly? I don't understand... you have space wings?"

She laughed. "No, like the blimp, only more advanced."

"Bullshit." He slowed, looked to see if she was serious, then shook his head and kept walking. "I don't know if I should believe you on half this stuff or—"

"No or," Robin said from behind. "Just believe her. It's your best chance for survival."

He grunted acknowledgement, but kept walking in silence for a moment after that.

Soon, they emerged into a narrow tunnel, where another group of pirates was just finishing attaching torches to the walls. The smoke was strong, but the room had ventilation and appeared to have once been a basement, judging by the old, rusty furnace in the corner and cracked concrete floor.

"The hell are they doing here?" one of the other pirates asked. She was tall and slender, with a crooked nose and scar across her cheek.

"Not taking sass from you, that's for sure," Cammie said with a growl.

"Back off, Toiya," Martha said, stepping up next to Cammie. "And you, try not to draw blood with the good guys."

"She's one of the good guys?" Cammie said with a laugh. "It's hard to tell around here."

"We're all pirates," Martha replied. "That's something you have to accept."

"Are you, though?" Robin asked, looking around at them with a frown. "I mean, I get that technically you are, but what's up with the costume party?"

"This coming from the girl wearing a ninja outfit under her pirate dress," Toiya said with a scoff.

Other pirates were starting to line up behind her, and it was looking like a showdown. If it continued like this, the whole idea of an underground operation would end in a bloodbath instead, and Valerie had experienced enough blood baths in her life to know she never wanted one of those again.

Sometimes death was inevitable, but not here like this.

"We've come to put a stop to the Prince," Valerie said. "And my friend here meant no disrespect."

"The hell I didn't," Cammie said, but in that instant Valerie turned on her, gripping her by the pirate vest she wore, and spoke at a level so quiet only her Were ears could pick it up.

"We're not here to kill 'em all, we're here to stop their piracy and bring as many of them as we can to our side. How do you propose to do that if they're dead?"

Cammie gritted her teeth, clearly not enjoying being addressed like this, but then smiled and pulled herself free from Valerie's grip.

"My apologies," Cammie said, with a hint of mockery that the pirate chose to ignore.

Valerie introduced them, then said, "And I'm Valerie. Vampire princess, liberator of New York, and now, apparently, superhero."

Toiya cocked her head at that, at a loss for words, and then started laughing. The other pirates behind her laughed, too, and soon they were all laughing. A distant yell silenced them, followed by an explosion and more gunfire.

"He's making a play," Martha said, glancing up at the dirt roof. "By now, that bastard Bairne and his men have reported what happened, so he's trying to teach you a lesson."

Valerie smiled, refusing to let bastards like the Prince get her down. "I was a good student, in my day. But I graduated, got myself a degree in Fuck-you, and now I think I'll give him a little education in return."

More hooting and hollering from the pirates, but this time Toiya held up her hands for silence.

"Don't go getting our hopes up like that," she said. "We've had supposed heroes try to put him down before. His head came back with a bow on it."

"Shit," Cammie said.

Robin nodded, as if that was normal.

"And there hasn't been an uprising against him?" Valerie asked.

River scoffed. "This lot?"

He leaped back as Martha moved to box his ears, but when he was on the other side of the room, standing beside a boy about his age, he smiled at the sight of her slowing. Valerie could tell by the look on this boy's face what was happening—he wasn't as friendly-looking as River appeared, not with the scruff on his neck and thick, hairy arms. He almost looked like a Were, she thought, if being buff and hairy actually had any correlation.

"What my stupid nephew is trying to get at," Martha said, "is that the Prince has too big a following. Anyone tries to make a move against him, they better come with a force. A force, we have not."

"I'm not following," Robin interjected. "Who was your leader before he came along?"

Toiya shook her head, glancing over her shoulder at the pirates, who had begun preparing themselves with food and opening crates of weapons. "Wasn't one. Pirates ain't meant to be led, not like regular folk, anyway. That's part of why we sail, because we crave the freedom of the open sea and skies. We live off of it… and now this son of a bitch is killing us."

"Figuratively and literarily," one of the pirates in the crowd behind her said.

"And here I was thinking that we were coming up here to kill you all," Cammie said with a chuckle that no one else shared. At a look from Royland she said, "What? You thought that, too, right? I mean, you were prepared at least, right?"

"Prepared to kill us all?" Toiya stared at her as if waiting for Cammie to laugh and say she was joking, but when that didn't happen she turned back to Martha and frowned. "Exactly what sorta scum did you bring here?"

"The powerful kind," Cammie said.

"The kind that are now on the same side as you," Valerie added. "It's not going to be like before."

"Fine, fine," Toiya said, waving her off and still glaring at Cammie. "But I'm still stuck on this kill us all thing. Who the hell are you and what the fuck?"

When Cammie looked to Valerie for help, Valerie simply smiled in a you-dug-your-own-grave kind of way.

"The pirates have been causing a lot of trouble for us down south," Cammie said. "And in this day and age, what's the best way to deal with a problem? Remove it, with lots of blood."

"I thought we were messed up," River's buddy said, his voice hoarse, like he'd been yelling too much.

"You are," Cammie replied. "But we don't take shit from anyone, and have the power to enforce this rule."

"And slavery?" Robin asked, her voice cool, not giving away any emotion.

Martha shook her head. "That hasn't reached out here yet, but the Prince certainly has connections to those involved out west."

Robin turned to Valerie and said, "Then it's settled. We do it your way here, then move. But we do it fast."

"Of course," Valerie replied. "I take care of my family, then help you take care of yours. The question is," she continued while turning to address the room, "where do I find this man?"

"The Prince?" Toiya scoffed. "Walk back outside, I'm sure he'll find you."

"Perfect," Valerie said, and then started walking.

"Wait, you're going to get torn to shreds." Toiya said, stepping between her and the exit. "I can't allow that."

"I wouldn't word it that way," Royland said with a chuckle. "You don't not allow Valerie to do anything."

"What, you go unchecked, is that it?" Toiya continued. "You're some tough murderess who gets to do whatever she wants, whenever she wants?"

"Toiya!" Martha stepped forward, finger pointed at the other woman. "Stand down!"

Toiya held her ground, though, fierce eyes staring at Valerie.

Finally, Valerie sighed and gave a shrug. "All I know is what I've been appointed to do, by a higher power than myself. In a way."

"From superhero to angel," Toiya said with a laugh.

"Do you want me to do something about this woman?" Cammie asked. "Something violent, preferably."

The pirates who had been pulling out weapons stood at that moment, odd guns and swords pointed at Cammie.

"No," Valerie said, frustration etching her voice. "From now on, we are one, got it? Everyone here will be working together to overthrow this bastard who calls himself a prince, and anyone who's not with us is against us. Is this understood?"

"And if I say fuck you?" a muscular man said, stepping forward from behind Toiya. "If I say this pirate's life is the life for me?"

"Try it, but make sure you say it close enough to kill me as the last words leave your mouth, because otherwise you'll find yourself missing a tongue, or worse."

"I'd personally love to hear him say it," Cammie said with a sneer. "And see what happens next."

"Stand down," Toiya said to her man. "Your wife certainly wouldn't complain if we had an out here."

The large man looked punched in the gut at that comment. He nodded, shot a glare Valerie's way and then said, "Fine, tell us what to do."

"Don't worry," Valerie replied. "Disposing of assholes is what I do best."

"It's kinda become her thing," Royland added.

"And she's really very good at it," Robin said. "I've seen it, first hand."

"That's all great," the man said, "but what does that actually mean?"

"We had planned on getting the lay of the land first, then going to find this guy and tear him a new asshole, but..."

"Now he knows someone's here, and he's been told what that someone did to his guys," Martha said.

"Exactly."

"Good news is that you all can simply fill us in on everything," Royland said. "Saving us a step."

"And the other pirates?" Robin asked.

"What do you mean?"

"They'd have to join us, right? I mean, after what he just did up there, shooting at them randomly. If there were an uprising, surely they'd join our side."

"You would think so," Toiya answered. "But a lot of our type see power as the only qualification for a leader. He does something like this, they don't take it personal."

"One of you puts a bullet in me," Cammie said with a scoff, "trust me, I'm taking it personal."

"Aye, but you aren't a pirate," the large man said, who had returned to counting ammo.

"Then we show them power," Valerie said. "But first, that woman's head."

"Wait, what?" Toiya frowned.

"I'm not letting it stay there."

"And if the Prince is up there right now, waiting for you?"

"Then he's as stupid as I hope he is." Valerie smiled, then turned to the door. "You all get the intel of this place, figure out a plan of attack so we can be out of here by morning, and then get to it."

"I'm coming with you," Robin said, but Valerie held up a hand. "I want as few targets as possible."

Robin looked about to protest, but Cammie chuckled and said, "Trust me, you can't win an argument with her," which was enough.

Valerie exited back out through the tunnels, considering this new situation she had found herself in. This wasn't like before, where she was liberating people from an overlord, or not exactly. Here it was more like a warlord, and many of his subjects were just as supportive of him as not.

She would have to show she was powerful in her own right, and not just take him down without considering their loyalty and how to snatch it up.

But first, she had to do this.

She pushed the door open and emerged into the night, where she saw the blimp, dark against the moon, heading back to a point near the old hotel. The night was silent now, aside from the occasional cry of pain from those who had been hit.

The area was foreign to her, but it was easy enough to walk back among the makeshift huts and figure out her route. A couple of the huts were in flames, and several injured pirates walking past glared at her.

Suddenly, something hit her leg, when she turned to look, thinking it was a rock or something, she saw a throwing dagger sticking out of her calf.

Then it clicked—this Prince character wasn't just showing off his power, he was sending the message that it was her fault they were suffering. They wouldn't look at him as the evil one here, but her.

She pulled the knife out, grunting in pain and annoyance, and then saw a flash of another blade coming her way. This one she side-stepped and, spotting the slender man who had attacked her, threw the knife back his way. It smacked him in the face and then bounced off and fell to sink into the earth.

"Shit," the man said, holding his nose where the blade's hilt had whacked him. "What kind of throw was that?"

"Throwing knives was always hit or miss for me," she said, then drew the double pirate swords her outfit demanded. "Slicing a man from ear to ear, that part I've got covered."

He stepped out of the shadows, another throwing knife at the ready, and said, "I coulda killed you with the first throw."

"You could've tried."

His brow furrowed at that, but he added, "I chose to send you a message instead. You need to leave this place."

Her swords felt light in her hands, as if they were begging her for blood, but she paused. "We'll be leaving, but only after ousting your leader."

The man spat on the ground, his lip twitching in disgust.

"So, not a true leader of yours, is he?" she asked.

"Just be gone. We don't need trouble from your sort."

She ignored that and turned to continue on her way, but said over her shoulder, "I have business here. If you annoy me again, you will die."

After a few moments, she heard his footsteps following, but he didn't cause any trouble. At the clearing where the scuffle had broken out earlier, she paused and looked back at him in the shadows, but he just stood there, staring back.

A glance around the clearing showed everyone had cleared out, or been cleared out. Streaks of blood still lined the ground, one moving toward the building where the woman's head was still impaled on a spike. One of those streaks led to a dark form moving along the ground ahead.

The man whose wife's head was up on that pole. He was pulling himself toward it, intent on reaching her no matter what.

Valerie approached and, when she was over him, said in a quiet voice, "Don't be alarmed. I'm going to help you."

With that she bent down, picked him up, and carried him forward. She smelled the scent of the men and women watching before she saw them, but as she reached the building where the head was, she saw at least a dozen pirates watching from the shadows. The man grunted, pointing as if she didn't know where he was trying to go.

Here she lifted him up and helped him, as if he was a small child, to stand at a position where he could grab the pole. He pulled at it, struggling to get it free, and she could hear the way he was holding back sobs.

"Allow me," she said, but he held up a hand.

"No, this is something I have to do," he said.

So, standing there supporting him, she waited as he grunted, pulling at the pole, rocking it back and forth until he finally wrenched it free. They climbed back down. The man tried to stand on his own, but was unable to.

"Where?" she asked, and he pointed to a spot down a decline and by a small stream. She carried him over and there he pulled the head from the pole, set it gently at his side, and then, on his knees, began digging into the ground with the pole. She shook her head, amazed at his determination.

"Can I at least help you here?" she asked.

He looked up, revealing tears that streaked through the blood caked on his face.

"You've done so much, thank you. But this part, I gotta do."

She nodded, understanding that, then noted several intimidating looking pirates moving their way. He looked up and saw them, too, and then hung his head.

"Them, I have no problem with you taking care of," he said, and then got back to digging.

"With pleasure," she replied, and drew her swords again.

She marched back up the slight hill, but noticed the slender man with the throwing knives among them, and paused.

"What's this?" she hissed when they were close enough to hear.

"This," the slender man said, motioning to the other man behind her, burying his wife's decapitated head. "We came because of this."

"If you try to stop him, I will stand in your way."

"We wouldn't dream of it. In fact, we want to offer our services."

"And what services would they be?" she asked.

"Mostly helping you against them," the man said, pointing over his shoulder to what Valerie hadn't noticed yet. Forms were starting to appear at the outskirts of the clearing and, as they spoke, they began filling the area. Pirates, every one of them.

"I don't need your help," she said. "But appreciate it nonetheless."

The man cocked his head at her, but nodded.

"Try to keep them off of this man," she said, already walking past them to the large group ahead, "at least until he's done burying what's left of his wife."

The group split, with a couple of them following her, one on each side, while the rest formed a semicircle of defense around the man as he dug.

Valerie smiled at this sign of camaraderie that she hadn't expected to find here, but she started running and, as the thought of her sword sinking into flesh or the feeling of steel scraping on bone entered her head, the smile was replaced with a snarl.

She was glad to see the enemy moving to attack first—it always made her feel that much less guilty for taking their lives when they struck first.

A crossbow bolt shot at them, nearly hitting the woman to Valerie's right, but Valerie slapped it aside with her sword and kept running. A man pulled out a pistol, another a rifle, and she decided there was no point in dragging this out.

Pushing fear, she let her eyes glow red and then used her vampire speed to rush forward. Before they could even pull their triggers, she was cutting off limbs, snatching out throats, and destroying them like they were paper cutouts.

The clash of steel and gunshots nearby told her the others had engaged in combat, too, and then there was yelling, and the fighting seemed to have stopped.

In front of her were two more pirates, but they were backing up, glancing between her and the others. The stench of death was strong in the night air that otherwise smelled of feces.

"They're abominations," one of the pirates was shouting, sword held out at the slender man's throat. "Every one of them needs to die. Especially her!"

The slender man simply smiled and said, "Halo's wife wasn't one, and even if she had been, you all had no right."

"We were given the right by the Prince!" the other said, and then charged.

The slender man took a slice on the side of his shoulder, but managed to duck under the other's second attack, come up behind him, and slit his throat.

As the man fell, the rest fled.

Only half of her support team of pirates remained, but they staggered over to their friend who, in spite of everything going on around him, was putting the final dirt over the burial spot.

"Now, which one of you sad bitches is gonna bury me?" the man said, sitting beside the grave and looking dead already.

"You're going to live on," the slender man said, wrapping an arm around his companion.

Valerie was frankly confused, but touched. She stood aside as the remaining pirates helped their friend to stand, and then started walking off with him.

"What will you do?" she called after them.

"Lie low until this thing between you and the Prince is over," the slender man said. "Meaning, until one of you is dead."

"You could join in the fight," she pointed out.

"We're thieves and cutthroats," he said. "We'll leave over-throwing gods to you."

She frowned, but realized it made sense. They were pirates after all. The fact the River kid and the others had offered to help should have been more surprising than the fact that these ones would go into hiding until it was all over.

With the man's wife buried and that taken care of, she strode off to return to the others and make their move.

CHAPTER THIRTEEN

Old Manhattan

By the time Sandra fell asleep in Diego's arms, he knew he'd be heading off on the mission soon. He kissed her, woke her gently to say he was leaving, and then took a quick shower before heading to the mess hall at Enforcer HQ for a coffee.

The night air was refreshing, a cool breeze sweeping through the city that reminded him of the streets back in Spain. It wasn't even that long ago, and yet it felt like another lifetime.

What was he getting himself into with this whole baby business? He had no clue. There had been a single mom that he knew when he was twelve, and she had it bad. It was up to him and his friends to help her get food for the little one, because nobody else would. And one day, she had left in search of the father. Memories of that child's wide eyes, full of confusion as they left, would never leave him.

That was the extent of his experience with children, and he had practically been a child himself. Now he was, what? A warrior in this new city? He sighed at losing himself in such thoughts as he continued on to HQ. Soon, he was going through the door and into the lobby, where he passed the guards who nodded, recognizing him without trouble.

When the elevator doors pinged open, he entered and nodded to two vampires who joined him. He didn't say anything, wanting to ride in silence until he had caffeine running through his body. It was funny how, as a Were, his body fought it off, but he loved the small kick it gave him anyway.

"You're the cat, huh?" one of the vampires asked.

Diego glanced over, analyzing the guy's leather jacket and short cropped beard. A wannabe tough guy, perhaps?

"That's you," the guy continued, "the one they say came over with Valerie?"

"Yup, Werecat they say, but I don't become a pussy, if that's what you're implying."

The vampire's eyes went wide. "Oh, damn, I mean, I didn't mean to imply that."

A chuckle escaped the other's mouth, and Diego considered hitting him. The guy must've noticed, because he covered his mouth and said, "Sorry, I just... hadn't thought of that. You're funny, man."

Diego blinked, not expecting that.

"A lot of people pick fights with you, or something?" the one with the leather jacket asked. "I mean, you seem a bit jumpy."

The other elbowed him and said, "Didn't you hear, he's having a kid."

"No shit?" the man held out his hand, and when Diego shook it, added, "Congrats, man. Huge congrats."

"Will it be a... Were?"

Both were staring at Diego. He bit his lip, pondering this, and then said, "I have no idea."

"If we had a kid, would it be a vampire?" the leather jacket man asked.

"We ain't having a kid," the other said. "Because I'm not into dudes."

"Wouldn't be anything wrong with it if you were," Diego said.

The vampire laughed. "Of course not. Me and that big, gay Were are super tight. I'm just saying I'm not having a kid with a dude."

"You mean Felix?" Diego asked.

"Yeah, he's been out there kicking butt on the training grounds."

"Thought the vampires and Weres were training separately?"

The vampire shrugged. "Sure, but we're not stupid. We know we'll be working together, and we know it's smart to be aware of the best ones, the ones we'll want at our backs."

"There's nobody better for getting your back than Felix," Diego said, smiling at the memory of that big guy saving him from captivity in the Golden City. "Oh, and I don't mean in some weird misinterpreted way of what I said. In case there is any."

"Hey, man, we wouldn't make jokes like that about him," the guy with the leather jacket said, then the doors dinged open. "Name's Platt, by the way."

"And I'm Bryant," the other said. "See you out there in a few?"

"You two on the mission?" Diego asked as he exited the elevator.

They both nodded.

"Diego. See you there." He nodded as the door closed, and turned to the mess hall. He was surprised to find it fairly crowded. He supposed it made sense, what with troops preparing for the mission, and others preparing to go out on patrol in the streets, in case anything went down while the others were out.

He'd taken no more than three paces in when Felix stepped into his path, arms wide, and said, "Speak of the devil?"

"Me?" Diego asked with a chuckle. "We were literally just talking about you."

"All good, I hope?" the man said with an oversized shrug.

"Mostly that you're the size of a mountain."

Felix laughed. "Show me a mountain that's my equal, and I'll say you're lying."

Diego nodded to the coffee and Felix walked over with him. "What's this I hear about some of the Weres being untrustworthy?"

"Your guess is as good as mine," Felix said. "If it's true, it ain't my people we gotta worry about."

"You golden boys are all under control?" Diego asked.

"Golden boys?" He raised an eyebrow. "Creative, I guess… but yeah, we're good. It's always been the girls I worried about. Harder for me to manipulate, you know."

"How about Esmerelda and Presley hanging around Mr. Boss-man?"

"Wait, what?"

Diego cocked his head. "You don't know?"

"I've been so busy training I haven't had time to notice things like that."

Diego poured his coffee. He wished there was something to use to make it not so bitter aside from sugar, but the best they'd been able to import from across the ocean was the coffee and some vanilla, and he wasn't a fan of changing up the natural taste. The first sip made him cringe, but the second was a thing of beauty.

He turned back to Felix and noted the look of worry in the big man's eyes. "That bad?"

"I don't know those two so well, but, I mean, they were both up there in the main leadership rings, and by that, we can assume they aren't as pure as one would hope."

"And maybe they're trying to reinstate themselves?"

Felix sucked in air from the corner of his mouth. "Let's be clear that I'm not saying we assume that of women trying to get power."

"Shut the fuck up, Felix," Diego said with a laugh. "Nobody is saying that. We're talking about these two specific Weres. Is this something I need to watch out for?"

Felix shrugged. "Might be. That's all I can give ya."

Diego nodded, considering this.

"Come on." Felix nodded to the side area. "We got a few minutes to kill before heading out, right? Hit up the table hockey?"

"The what?"

"We put up this table and got two pucks. Some old dude used to go on about it in the Golden City, said it was this old game people would play. Figured we could use it here to ease the tension between missions. I'll go easy on you."

"Oh, you don't need to do that," Diego said. "I'm a quick learner."

They had a good game and Diego, though indeed a quick learner, had no shot at all at winning. Not that it mattered once they were on the road, weapons strapped over their shoulders, with Diego glancing back at the building where Sandra slept.

He had to be careful on this one—it was the first time he was heading off to a fight knowing that, if he never came back, he would leave behind a woman and their baby.

CHAPTER FOURTEEN

Isle of the Prince, Hotel

The Pirate Prince stared out at the revelry in his old hotel courtyard, men and women in each other's arms, two nude in a corner where they must've thought no one could see. Or maybe they knew he could see, and were giving him a private show.

He laughed, raising a glass of homemade rum, the only kind available these days, and took a swig. Those in the room behind him followed suit, he knew, but continued to watch the two below. Damn, that was hot. He'd have to find himself one of the newer pirate wenches for himself, but only after a couple more drinks of this horrible rum.

It burned in his throat, but gave him the strength needed to act the part he'd taken on for himself. Leader of the pirates... their prince, the Prince, as it were. He'd taken the name from what a local had said the island was called, Prince something or other island. He didn't really care about the history of it all, but thought it sounded cool.

A man who had lost his family to the whackos who roamed the night, he swore to never let anyone close again, and decided he would be surrounded by power at all times. If anyone was killing from now on, it was him and his.

He took another swig, shuddered as the vile liquid soaked into his innards and warmed his bones, and looked out at his small pirate army. Past the fucking, a team of them were tossing about some outsider they had found wandering too close to the island. They had likely dragged him back through the waters and, since he had somehow survived, taken to playing games with him. Games that involved dodging bullets and the pointy ends of their swords.

If the newcomer survived long enough and proved himself, he might even be invited to join the pirate ranks. To refuse meant death, to accept meant a lifetime of glory and riches.

It was like that here, with the groups he kept closest. Whatever the hell they wanted to do, he allowed, as long as they did it in his name. He would maintain order through terror.

There were groups among the pirates who lived normal lives, sure. He allowed it, in part because he believed some semblance of civilization gave what they were doing legitimacy, but also because he would look at those innocent eyes and see those of his son, before the whackos had ended his joy forever.

A glance into his cup told him it was empty, and he smiled.

When he turned, a room full of men and women paused their drinking and groping to await his orders.

"The fuck's everyone so gloomy about?" he asked. "Did I say to stop enjoying yourselves?"

Nervous glances told him they were too cowardly to make assumptions, so he pulled out a pistol, shot a hole in the ceiling, and said, "Get back to partying, you group of melon-sucking rat shits."

He didn't care if the insult didn't make sense, he figured it sounded pirate enough. Besides, the rum was making his head swim, and he was feeling good. He motioned to the nearest pirate woman, one named Jessabel, if he remembered correctly, and she practically leaped off of ol' Kedrick's lap.

"Prince?" she asked, eyes hopeful.

"You'll do," he said, and started walking to his chambers—an old converted suite in the hotel.

Gun shots went off outside, followed by hooting and hollering, and he smiled to himself. He fucking loved this little oasis of debauchery he'd created here. It was almost enough to make him forget the pain.

Almost.

He glanced back at the woman's large breasts, already exposed as she dropped her dress to the floor before the door was even closed. She turned to close the door, revealing the backside he now vaguely remembered slapping while going at her once or twice in the past, or, hell, who knows—maybe it'd been a few dozen times.

His eyes were rolling as she started to undo the lace that held up his britches, and he ran a hand through her wavy brown hair, preparing to pull her head in. Control. That's what it was all about, and he meant to remind himself of that tonight.

Which was why his anger flared when the door burst open and Captain Bairne came barging in, dripping blood on his new rug that he'd stolen from one of the supply ships.

"Prince, sir, I…" Captain Bairne's eyes darted down to the woman, then up to the Prince, and his face went pale. "Fuck me, I'm sorry, I…"

The Prince swatted Jessabel's hand aside and pulled his pants back up to cover himself, not sure if he should be more upset or less because he hadn't been fully aroused yet.

"You already interrupted," the Prince said, glaring. "Spit it out."

Bairne glanced down at the woman, waiting.

"Not her, you donkey-brained fuck," the Prince said, only finding a moment's humor in the situation. At least rum gave him that, sometimes. A reason to smile. "Bairne, why the hell are you bleeding on my rug, and what could be so important that you burst in on me like this?"

"Sorry again, Sir. Your highness." Captain Bairne hobbled forward, dreadlocks hanging around his head as the light from above cast a shadow that gave him the look of a demon coming to deliver the devil's message. "There's a newcomer... the one we've heard tales of from down south. She's here."

The Prince cocked his head at that, waved Jessabel away without a second glance, and then smiled.

"Well, hell boy." He aimed his pistol at Bairne, ran his tongue along his teeth to taste the remnants of rum still lingering there, and cocked the pistol. "Why isn't she dead?"

"The stories... they're true."

There was a moment where the Prince nearly pissed himself, thinking of the devil incarnate coming to his door step. He had his pirates hunting more than just whackos—creatures of the night were extra prized, their killers given extra reward. And now the ultimate of them, from the stories he had heard, was here at his home.

Well, good.

He had the chance now to prove himself once and for all. And if not? Well, at least his suffering would come to an end. An idea hit him, causing him to stand up tall and proud.

"Captain Kaine will deal with her," the Prince said. "We have nothing to worry about."

"Kaine is powerful," the captain admitted, glancing back into the other room nervously, where his followers had joined the others to see what was happening. "But he hasn't returned yet."

"Well, fuck a duck," the Prince replied with a chuckle. "Do we have to do all the hard work ourselves? Ready my air ship, and we'll see how many holes we can put into this she-devil before she collapses."

"And the settlement, your highness?" Bairne asked.

"They can't expect to live forever," the Prince said with a chuckle, then felt a surge of warmth downstairs and a bulge pressing against his pants and glanced around, looking for Jessabel. He saw her at the far end of the room, nearly dressed. "Not so fast, you."

She smiled and bit her lip, letting the dress fall again.

Bairne cleared his throat nervously, and the Prince turned to get some pre-slaughter enjoyment.

"I'll just… ready the air ship then," Bairne said, slowly backing out of the room.

"You don't have her ready by the time I'm finished here, I'll see that you're this she-devil's first victim," the Prince said, pulling Jessabel close. He pressed his mouth to hers and tasted sweet cherry tobacco, ignoring whatever Bairne was saying about how there'd already been a first. He didn't care, right now he was lost in the moment, lost in the flesh, and amped up with the thought of the oncoming slaughter.

Something had snapped in him that day long ago, the day he'd gone pirate. He knew it in a blurred way, like watching someone you know through a stained glass window, or like hearing someone call your name from far away. The knowledge was there, but it wasn't.

And at this point, he'd done enough evil to not want to remember who he had once been. At this point, it was all or nothing, and if he was being honest with himself, nothing sounded just great.

But until someone brought him to that point, he'd damn sure take all. He meant to start with Jessabel, and then move on to this she-devil.

Maybe she would learn to worship him like the rest of these peons, he thought, if he was merciful enough to let her live.

Prince Edwards Island, Tunnels

Shouting carried through the tunnels as Valerie approached, with one side shouting that there was no way in hell they were going to attack the Prince of Pirates until sunrise, when they suspected any dark powers he had vanished.

Robin, for her part was yelling about how they had delayed enough, and that if they didn't get moving on this soon, she would just leave them to do it on their own. Cammie and Royland took up her side of the argument, but were focusing on the point that Royland, too, would lose his advantage in the daylight.

"You can regenerate!" Martha said as Valerie entered. The woman's back was to her, but she sensed everyone else silencing, so she paused, and then turned. "Oh, you're back. Good. Everything settled out there?"

"His wife is buried, and he's with his friends." She joined Robin to lean against the wall, folding her arms across her chest. "Though there're more dead pirates out there now."

"What'd you do?" Toiya asked, her voice harsh.

"Helped a man in need. A man who'd been the victim of injustice."

"And that meant more killing?"

Valerie nodded. "That's what happens when people come at me or one of mine with the intention of seeing us harmed."

Toiya rubbed her temples, then said, "Well, I'm glad we're on your side."

"Great. Oh, and we attack immediately." Several mouths opened to protest, but Valerie continued, "The longer we wait, the greater the chance is that this bastard has hurt more people. That, and we have slavers to stop out west. Anyone who's scared can stay, but the rest of us make our move now. Got it?"

Nobody protested.

"You have a plan then?" Robin asked.

"Sure do. I'm going to walk up to his door, say I'm here for him, then commence to end his life on this glorious planet. Sweet and simple."

"Except that he'll take to the blimp the moment you make your move," Martha said. "And no other blimp can stand against his. So, unless you can fly…"

"If he sees her coming, that's true," River said, thoughtful.

"He'll have eyes everywhere at this point," Martha protested. "Sure, maybe that fast vampire movement thing she does might help, but other than that, I'm at a loss."

"What about the canals?"

Everyone turned to River with interest.

"Go on," Martha said.

River's eyes lit up. "We use the canals to get out to the ships. Then we just have to find an incoming one, and Valerie can make her way from the ship as it's unloading as if she were simply one of the crew. There happens to be a ship due tonight, and it's running late."

"It'll add the element of surprise," Martha said, nodding. "I don't care how tough you are, charging into a Gatling gun and an arsenal of pirates can't be fun."

"I wouldn't worry about it," Robin said with a distracted gaze.

"I've done worse," Valerie said in agreement. "But the difference there was that my goal was to kill the CEOs of Old Manhattan. My aim here is to overthrow a pirate Prince and, at the same time, win people to my side."

She thought about it for a moment, then said, "What if we intercepted the crew and convinced them to go along with us… then we all make as if we were delivering his cargo."

"We take a little schooner out there while they're doing the inventory," Martha leaned in, seemingly into the plan now, "and no one's the wiser."

"Whose vessel is it?" River asked.

"That's the problem," Toiya said. "Captain Kaine."

The room fell silent.

"And why's that a problem?" Cammie asked. "It seems we've missed something."

"Captain Kaine's probably the most vile of 'em all," River said. "He's brought in more plunder than the rest of the nine captains combined, and who knows how many heads he's had to take to get him there."

"We kill him and take his ship," Cammie replied. "Easy."

"He's the reason I'm still alive," Toiya replied, teeth clenched.

"Same goes for many here," Martha offered. "Truth is, you make a move on him, you've lost the loyalty of most of the men and women on the island."

"You have a better solution?" Valerie asked.

"Simply partner with him," Martha replied, but Valerie sensed a change in the woman, a look in her eye that said she had more to offer on the subject.

"Fine," Valerie said. "Everyone who's with us, prepare. Since the four of us aren't exactly experienced in taking boats—"

"Ships," Toiya corrected her.

"Okay, ships… We can provide the muscle, but we'll need your know-how."

"Aye aye," Toiya said, more mockingly than anything else, and turned to address her crew.

Martha stepped up next to Valerie and lowered her voice. "Shit happens."

Valerie frowned, unsure where to go with that. "Yes… it does."

"And if it happened to the captain while we were completing this mission," Martha paused to wink, as if that was necessary, "well, I doubt there'd be too many questions asked."

"Noted," Valerie replied with a nod. She wasn't sure she would judge this man by the word of a bunch of pirates, but so far, this group seemed better than the rest.

"I'll get ready, we should head out soon." Martha walked off to join Toiya and the others, who were changing into a stash of even more elaborate pirate clothes, complete with large hats, frills, and all.

Royland and Cammie had walked back up the hallway to have a chat, though Valerie wondered if it was more—those two were like dogs in heat. When it wasn't disgusting, it was actually sweet.

Valerie joined Robin at the entryway, where she seemed to be standing guard.

"You sure you're up for this?"

A flash of confusion creased Robin's brow. "Of course. I was trained for this."

"I mean, you're not… distracted?"

Robin smiled. "I'm always distracted. That hasn't stopped me in the past."

"Yes, but have you actually done much of this in the past?"

"I was fighting right alongside you," Robin said. "On more than one occasion, actually."

"Yeah, but—"

"Oh my God, you're worried about me!" Robin stared, mouth open, then said, "You're actually worried about me."

"It's not that I think you can't take care of yourself, I know you can. I just… don't want you to get hurt."

"Thanks, Val." Robin turned to walk away. "Your confidence in me is overwhelming."

Valerie grabbed her by the arm and spun her back. "I told you, it's not that. Listen, if anything happens to you, your family will be stuck in slavery. Nobody else knows what they look like. It's all on you. I know that's a lot to worry yourself about."

The two stood there, staring each other down, and then Robin leaned in, delicately, and placed her lips against Valerie's, gently, never once closing her eyes. When she pulled back, Valerie leaned forward with the departing lips, as if that would keep them together, but Robin was leaning away now, lips pursed and a very confused look in her eyes.

"That's what you wanted, right?"

Valerie licked her lips, confused. "I didn't not want it."

"Come on, I know how you look at me."

"You don't look back?"

That caused Robin to pause, but then she shrugged. "The point is that's out of the way now. No more wondering if it's going to be the most amazing feeling that either of us has ever experienced, because it's done. We're here to focus on two things, and neither of those allow for us playing it safe."

Valerie wanted to argue, to tell her that, yeah, it was one of the most amazing feelings of her life, those soft lips barely touching hers. Instead, she nodded, gulping down her words and stuffing her emotions into a box that would only be opened when she saw the pirates overthrown and Robin's family rescued.

"I..." Robin's gaze took on a distant look and she looked vulnerable for a moment, but then whatever she was about to say was gone, and the firm stare returned. "Now, let's get this over with."

"Agreed," Valerie said, but before Robin could turn away she said, "And then we're doing that again."

Robin bit her lip, trying to hide the smile, and then walked off. Valerie was about to join her, when she saw Cammie in the shadows watching with a huge grin.

"Oh, shit," Valerie said, trying to walk past her.

"You're not getting off that easy," Cammie said, matching her stride. "You never told me you were a rug muncher."

"A what?"

"You know." She nodded ahead to Robin. "But... what about Jackson? How do you explain that?"

"Shut up, Cammie. You're one to talk."

"Oh, I don't deny my sexual promiscuity and openness to trying new flavors. You want to know what happened with Esmerelda and Presley behind closed doors? Shit, find us a side room, and I'll show you right now."

"Cammie!" Valerie hit her, gently, but apparently it hurt

because Cammie yelped and pulled back, the smile fading for a moment. "Sorry."

"No, girl, play rough. I like that, too."

"I will seriously shut you up if you don't do it yourself." Valerie stepped forward, threateningly. "You doubt it?"

"Okay, okay, you're touchy when it comes to your relationships, I get it." Cammie stood there, trying not to smirk, but unable to help it. "What's wrong, Jackie-boy didn't bring the O?"

"Cammie…"

Cammie folded her arms and cocked her head to the side, waiting.

"God…" Valerie looked around to ensure no one was listening. "Okay, he was amazing, but it just didn't work out. Now, I feel things, right? It's not different or better, I can't explain it. It's just I felt something for him then, realized it can't be, and feel something for her now. Can it be? Probably not, but for now… we'll see."

"Damn, I was hoping it was just some sexual thing," Cammie said with a look of disgust. "Not all this touchy-feely stuff."

"Oh, and you and Royland aren't all lovey-dovey?"

Cammie blushed. "Homeboy brings it. And when I mean he brings it, I mean…" She held up her hands, a good distant apart, but Valerie waved her off.

"No, not like that."

"Oh…" Cammie rolled her eyes. "Yes, we're serious, okay. More serious than I've ever been. I don't wanna talk about it."

"What? Why?"

"That kinda stuff's personal."

Valerie just stared, mouth open. "THAT kind of stuff is personal?"

Cammie shrugged. "Yeah, I mean… sex stuff's like whatever. It's physical, anyone can do it. But this internal stuff? No one has to see it. Not that many people even experience it, right? So… personal."

Valerie couldn't believe it, but the woman was actually kind of making sense. "Okay, but that doesn't mean I'm going to start describing Jackson's manhood to you. Same goes with Robin's womanhood, if that ever happens."

"Tell you what," Cammie offered, leaning in conspiratorially, "you don't ask me about the internal stuff, I won't ask you about the physical."

"Deal." Valerie looked along the corner and saw Royland and Robin there with several others behind them, swords gleaming in the faint light. "What do you say we go kick some pirate butt?"

"I say they better have big ol' butts, because I plan on doing lots of kicking."

"You're weird, Cammie. As long as you know that."

"I wouldn't have it any other way."

Valerie laughed. "Me neither."

They continued on, and the others simply nodded, Robin avoiding Valerie's gaze, and then they all headed out through the tunnel. Valerie found her heart racing at the idea of getting to play dress up and infiltrate a group of pirates. It would be fun, she thought, to attempt subterfuge for once, instead of simple brute force.

CHAPTER FIFTEEN

Isle of the Prince, Hotel

"Where is she?" the Prince demanded, his head already starting to pound. Not only had Bairne not returned with news of a dead or captured she-devil, but Jessabel had failed to bring him to finish. As far as he was concerned, the world was imploding around him. "You can be damn sure that if I go down, I'm taking all you fucks with me."

The room of pirates simply stared and, as he walked past them, he noticed one of his lieutenants still had his pants down. They all stood as the Prince entered, apparently not taking the time to make themselves presentable.

With the pounding in his head and the frustration of this lack of good news, the Prince found his arms shaking.

As the pirate bent to pull up his trousers, the Prince caught him by the hair, drew his short-blade, and slit the man's throat.

"Is this how you present yourselves before royalty?" he demanded, dropping the pants-less, still shaking, dying man to the floor. "You scum, do any of you have a clue where you'd be without me?!"

The rest just stared at him, not a one of them able to answer that.

"Nowhere," he finally said in almost a whisper, then sunk into his throne—a wicker chair adorned with strings of ears and fingers he had collected over the years.

Jessabel cleared her throat, standing among the others. He pointed at her with the knife, still furious about earlier, and said, "What?"

She nodded to the window, and said, "There's something… you ought to see."

He sneered, exposing his teeth in a near growl, and wanted to plunge his knife into her. At least something to get a real reaction out of her.

But the alcohol was making him drowsy now, so instead of using the energy, he let his head roll to look toward the window. The sight there nearly sobered him up, and in an instant he was standing, moving to the balcony, and throwing open the door.

"Captain Kaine," he said, recognizing the captain's ship. "Well, then."

"Your highness," Jessabel said, glancing toward a man who the Prince didn't recognize. "This man is from Kaine's crew. He said they've all abandoned ship, that Kaine doesn't stand a chance. That…" She stopped, stared at the man, and then her expression hardened.

"That we're all royally fucked," the man said.

Anger flared in the Prince and he spun, letting the blade fly so that it slammed into the man's chest. Apparently, Kaine's crew hadn't been taught how to behave before royalty.

Well, that would be lesson one.

As he kicked the man over and bent to retrieve his blade, it hit him. A wave of dizziness came over him as he realized the man was right. If this woman was able to stand against Kaine, if his own crew lost faith in him when up against her, none of them stood a chance.

They had to retreat. They had to go for reinforcements.

They had to reach Toro and hunker down. But first, they'd crew-up at Slaver's Peak. Yes, that was the only way.

"Ready my ship and my escort," the Prince said. "We're not going down without a fight. You can count on that."

Isle of the Prince, Slums

Moonlight shone on them, low in the sky in a way that showed the night would soon be over. Eyes followed the group of two-dozen or so pirates, eyes of watchers who knew that the recent shooting was likely related to these pirates. Who else would be out on a night like this, and who else in such numbers?

When they had passed through the bit of a village, if you could call it that, and were approaching the far shore on the other side of the island, the sound of a distant banjo carried through the night, and Valerie got the distinct feeling of a place she had visited once in her early days of being a vampire, an old theme park long ago destroyed. It had a part to it that felt like a permanent night-time, but was indoors, and there, too, had been a character with a banjo.

She had hung out there with a couple of the junior vampires once, each taking turns trying to recall the old days, the days before the Duke had taken them under his wing.

And then Donovan had found them, him and his goons, and they'd smashed that place up, beat the hell out of the young vampires—all but Valerie, who they made to watch while they did it.

The day that bastard had died was a truly monumental day for this world.

It had almost gone too far, when one of those asses, the large one who had sat in the corner plucking at the banjo, came for her and tried to do more than make her watch. She still remembered the look in his eyes as he reached for her, and then the way his nose had collapsed into his face at the strike from Donovan.

She almost would've considered Donovan a brother at that moment if not for what had come after.

"No one touches her but me," he said, though he never did. Still, the idea of him claiming ownership of her threw off any positive thoughts she might have otherwise had in that moment.

Then a thought hit her... That vampire, he had been with Donovan on the blimps, but she never actually saw him die. Could it be possible? She turned to the sound of the banjo, considering the idea that the Prince could actually be that vile creature.

Timing wise, it added up. And then there was the banjo, though that was a loose connection. Was it possible that the vampire had always had an affinity for pirates, so sought them out after fleeing from what would have otherwise been his death? She had a good feeling that the answer to that was yes.

Now, more than ever, she wanted to be able to sneak in there and confront him in a way that he would never suspect.

Then she'd grab him by the throat and tear it out for even thinking of her in a negative context involving harm.

"You focused?" Robin asked, joining her as they climbed into a small boat alongside River and Martha. A 'schooner' they called it.

"As focused as I'll ever be."

Soon, River and Martha, with the help of a couple others who joined them, had the boat in action. The plan was simple—get out to the other boats, one that was unoccupied, then hail the incoming vessel as if they had recently returned, and offer help. Since Valerie had no clue how all this pirate stuff worked, she had no choice but to shrug and assume the plan was sound.

The schooner made its way across the water, slowly, and she couldn't help but be amazed at the ships anchored ahead. These were big ships, two or three masts to each one, and a bunch of that rigging stuff going on—all sorts of beams and sails that she imagined she would never know the names of, and probably never would need to, if not for the fact that she was playing the part of a pirate right now.

"Don't worry," Martha said, glancing over and seeing the look in her eyes. "Not many of us know a thing about these ships, either."

"How do you sail them then?" Robin asked.

River laughed. "There're just a few sailors, trying to teach the rest of us. Most of us function as either fighters or pack-mules, though."

"You all made these ships?" Valerie asked, not even trying to hide the awe in her voice.

"Not exactly," Martha said, steering the schooner toward one of the smaller ships. "Though, there were some crews from out west that came here to put a couple together. Mostly fix up jobs, a lot of the labor from..." Martha paused, glancing at Robin.

"Slaves," Robin said, finishing the sentence for her.

Martha nodded.

"No more questions," Valerie said, zipping her mouth. "You lead, we follow."

"Just stick close, make like you're being useful."

"But don't appear too strong," River said. "It'll make them suspicious of you."

"One more question, actually," Robin said, leaning forward anxiously in the boat. "When it comes to killing these sons of bitches, can you repeat what you just said? You know, about the slaves thing."

Valerie frowned, but didn't ask. Martha, however, just had to. "Why?"

Robin clutched her sword hilt. "So that I won't feel bad about killing any of them."

A whistle sounded from ahead, and Martha held up a hand, then pointed. Out of the darkness, to the point that Valerie was surprised the others could even see it, a large ship was slowly approaching.

As it became more clear, Valerie had to suck in her breath in awe. That thing was a beast—literally, the front of it was curved with thick plating, the likeness of a beast's face on it.

The sails rippled in the wind as the ship came about, and even from this far away, it was majestic to behold.

"Quick, climb aboard," Martha commanded, and sure enough, the other schooners were unloading onto this ship and the one nearby. They went about moving ropes and whatnot, so that by the time the massive ship came to, the charade was in full force.

As they had discussed, the incoming ship soon put to anchor. Martha hailed them and offered their services, saying they had just finished unloading their own ship and were ready to come aboard if the other crew could use the help. They were waved over, gratefully.

They climbed aboard, and for the first time in a while, Valerie actually felt that going into the lion's den style of nervous.

"Who's the fresh fish?" a bald pirate with dark skin asked as they boarded.

"Newbies from out west," Martha replied. "You got a big haul?"

The guy gave them a quick glance, didn't seem to think much of them, and pointed to the opposite side of the ship. Sure enough, there were several wooden crates of the type Valerie knew had likely been destined for New York, or possibly meant for going on westwards, out to TH and his crew in Chicago, maybe. Either way, they didn't belong to these pirates, and that bothered her.

It almost bothered her to the extent that she would pull out her sword and dole out justice. But no, for once Michael's enforcer of justice would stay quiet in favor of justice down the line of a greater variety—taking out the Prince.

Or whatever the hell the name was of that bastard friend of

Donovan's. She racked her brain as she tried to appear weaker than she was, helping Royland and Cammie, who had joined them now, too, pretending to be a crew from another ship, lift a crate and carry it to the edge to lower over the side of the ship.

The doors banged open behind them and Valerie noticed several eyes dart up and then away just as fast... back to their work.

She was willing to bet that was Captain Kaine who had just exited. He would lead them to the Prince, to... wait a minute, she spun, realizing something.

"The fuck you doing on my ship, girl?" The large man, built like a bulldog with his scrunched up nose and broad, meaty soldiers, loomed over them, glaring right at her.

Yup, this plan had rapidly gone to shit. It was time to go with plan B, before she got the good pirates—or at least the pirates who were on her side—hurt.

"Kaine," she said, the name and all of those memories came flooding back to her. He wasn't the Prince, but was apparently either putting up with someone taking the leadership role, or using that someone as a puppet. "I've come for a reckoning."

"Kill her," he said, and turned as if it would be so simple.

She laughed, and as a wave of pirates appeared, pistols and swords aimed in at her, she pushed out with fear. These weren't soldiers. These weren't even really battle-hardened pirates, as it wasn't like there was a royal navy of old to put up a fight. And so they buckled, some soiling their pants right there, others jumping overboard.

And then she took a step forward, letting her eyes glow red, so that more of them went running for their lives.

All, that is, but for a handful of Kaine's followers. The ones she had guessed were vampires, though the salt of the sea hid their scent.

"You messed up my playtime," she said. "I had so been looking forward to having my pirate time."

"It doesn't have to end here," he said, pulling a pistol and a cutlass. "Maybe I cleave you in two and leave you to be eaten by the fish. That sounds rather like a pirate-thing, wouldn't you say?"

She laughed, glancing at Robin and the others and hoping they would stay back. "Tell you what. Maybe we do it like the old captains? A duel, winner takes the ship."

"First, you have no ship to give up," Kaine said, scowling. "Second, I don't think that's how the old pirates did it."

"But you don't know, do you?"

He glared, then descended down the stairway with thunderous steps.

"You sure about this, Val?" Cammie asked.

Valerie was caught off guard by that. "Um, haven't you seen what I'm capable of?"

"Sure, but… he's a big ass dude."

Kaine laughed. "Little piratita has a point. Last chance to run with your tail between your legs, bitch."

"Didn't your mommy ever tell you not to use that word?" Valerie asked, and didn't wait for a response before diving into the attack.

She had pretty much only ever used the large European-style sword she had grown accustomed to, but that was back on the blimp with Captain Bronson, so she would have to learn how to use these pirate swords fast. They were thinner, with a slight curve. As she brought one attack after another at Kaine, she began to appreciate these blades. She could move faster than she ever had with the claymore, and she imagined she looked damn cool doing it.

Even with her skills and speed, hitting him was hard though. For one, he was much quicker than his size would suggest, and even though she was strong, that didn't mean she had the perfect sense of balance. When he caught her off-guard, she went toppling over.

That's when his minions leaped in to join the fight, and he did nothing to stop them.

Valerie found herself covered in vampires, some trying to scratch with claws or strike with blows, others brandishing weapons and trying to get clean shots.

"Forget this," Robin said, and came in swinging her sword in Valerie's defense. Her moves caught Kaine's eye and, as Valerie killed one vampire after another, she couldn't help but notice him staring at Robin in a very lustful way.

So it was that she took great pleasure in killing the last vampire and then taking Robin's hand for a slight squeeze. It was enough to tell him she was off limits. Not that it would matter, since he'd be dead soon, Valerie thought. Still, couldn't let him die thinking he could have accomplished more in life than was realistic.

"That's how it's done!" Cammie said, tossing a pirate overboard who had apparently attempted to attack her. Now it was just their friendly pirates, them, and Kaine.

"What are you even doing here?" Kaine asked, eyes now showing that he finally understood the predicament he was in.

He took a step back, pistol pointed at her chest. She advanced.

"You couldn't just let me have it?" he asked. "Your damned quest for revenge demands you hunt us all down until it's completely over, is that it?"

"Not at all," she said, feeling the balance of her swords as she advanced. "You could've retired to a hut on the shore, lived out your life eating fish and sucking the blood of chickens, but instead you became not only part of the problem, but, from what I hear, a major pillar of the problem. I mean to watch you all collapse, until the roof comes tumbling down."

"I should've taken you that night, after Donovan turned his back." The man took a step toward her now. "I could've, you know. You were weak then, just like you're weak now." At a push of fear from her, his eyes widened, but he didn't back down. "Oh, maybe not physically or with this magic or whatever you want to call it, but mentally? You're just the same young, stupid vampire you were back then."

"Oh, cut out his throat and jam it into his eye socket," Cammie said. "Stupid prick."

"This one's asking for trouble," Kaine said, turning his attention on her.

"Nuh-uh," Valerie said, stepping between the two. "You're my kill."

"Uh, guys," Martha shouted from the rear of the ship. The others all looked, but Valerie had to keep her attention on the man before her. Out of the corner of her eye, she saw what they were all looking at—a dark form rising up from past the tall building they had been aiming for earlier.

"That's the Prince's air ship," River said, and this time Valerie glanced up to see one massive airship, flanked by three more all with their Gatling guns at the ready. For a moment she thought that it was coming for them, but then it started veering off toward the land to the west.

"The hell…?" she started to ask, but a flash went off at her side, and a bullet tore through her cheek. Dammit, that hurt.

As she was coughing up blood, she turned in time to see Kaine's cutlass as he swung it for her head. She brought up both swords to block the strike and push it aside, and was glad she did, too, because the force knocked her backward. If it had hit her, it could've cleaved her in two.

"You want the slavers, you need the Prince," Toiya shouted and made her move to attack Kaine from behind, he was quick, but Valerie was quicker. As he turned to dodge Toiya's blow and then shoot her point blank, Valerie thrust one of her swords, connecting with the arm and driving into his chest.

He groaned, staggering back, but then pulled the sword out and tossed it to clank across the deck.

Behind him, the large man from the pirate tunnels collapsed, and Toiya screamed, running for him.

This son of a bitch just made their situation worse, because now Valerie decided she was going to have to let that woman take the final blow.

When he lunged with his good arm, Valerie was there with a strike, and she sent the arm flying with a swift, clean cut right through the bicep.

"No healing from that, asshole," she said, and then clocked him with the hilt of her sword right on the nose.

He fell backwards and onto his butt, dark blood pouring out over his face.

"You won't catch him," Kaine said. "Nobody flies this ship but me, and since I'm about to die…"

"Wait, fly this ship?" she glanced over to Martha, who nodded. "This ship turns into a blimp?"

Martha nodded, but motioned to Kaine. "I think we can figure it out, but first, do you mind?"

"Actually, I think someone else should get to do it." She walked forward and kicked Kaine back so that he lay flat on the deck, then stabbed her sword downward and into his good arm, so that he was pinned there.

He shouted in pain and anger, spitting at her, but she simply stepped back and waited.

Finally, Toiya looked up, catching on.

She was too furious to smile, but a hint of excitement at the idea of being the one responsible for bringing him to justice shone in her eyes.

When Valerie saw that the woman held a machete, she was about to intervene and ask someone to lend her a sword, but it was quickly clear that was unwanted. Toiya went to town on the vampire, hacking and slashing and loving every shout of pain or gurgle of blood from him. The rest either watched or turned away from it all. When it was over and Toiya sat there, covered in blood, a dead vampire before her, Martha told Valerie that the two, Toiya and the large man, had some on-again-off-again relationship.

She suspected something of the sort.

Just to be certain, she walked up to Toiya's side, took the machete, and gave the neck of Kaine's corpse one last chop, separating it from the body. Next, she took both and tossed them overboard.

That out of the way, she looked to Martha and said, "Get this ship into the air."

Martha nodded and began shouting orders, and soon, they were pulling aside trap doors and pulling levers, then disconnecting masts, so that the inner part of the ship actually disconnected from the outer hull. Beneath them was a separate deck, this one with a large balloon waiting to be inflated.

"This is insane," Valerie said, shaking her head.

"Greater things were accomplished at the expense of slaves," Robin said.

"God, you're a downer." Valerie bit her lip, nodding. "And soon, all that will be taken care of."

"How...?" Cammie asked, staring at the disappearing blimps. "Captain Bairne must've told them we're coming, right?"

"He might've been ready to move anyway," Martha offered. "Doing a delivery run, bringing slaves out here, even. That's the rumor I've heard, anyway. Could be coincidence, or could be he decided to make his move earlier when he heard about you all."

The group soon had the balloon up and beginning its inflation process, but Cammie and Royland were discussing something. Valerie nodded at them and cleared her throat.

Cammie glanced over, hesitated, then said, "We've been thinking."

"What about Captain Bronson?" Royland asked, watching the blimp fill with hot air.

"And this place," Cammie added, glancing around. "We leave

them now, who's to say they don't just revert back to the way they were under the Prince?"

"Sounds like you're going somewhere with this, Cam?" Valerie asked.

"I'm just saying. If you all go take out the Prince, and this Kaine guy is pretty much gone, these people will need leadership, someone to keep them in line."

"And that someone would be?"

Cammie shrugged. "Maybe me?"

"Maybe us," Royland cut in.

For a moment, the two looked at each other, and then Cammie grabbed his hand and squeezed. "Maybe... us."

Valerie couldn't help but laugh. "Only you two have the ability to be romantic on a pirate ship covered in guts and gore."

"So, that's a yes?"

"You're right, after all." Valerie watched the balloon inflate, observing the pirates going about their tasks. "These men and women, they aren't evil. They just need direction. We'll pursue the ship, put an end to this piracy, and leave you two to ensure the eastern hub of their operations is no more. New York will trade with you, or we'll figure out some sort of system, but piracy will not be part of it."

"How about the clothes," Cammie said, twirling in her pirate dress. "We can still wear these, right?"

Royland chuckled. "I'm going to make damn sure you do."

"Oh, is that right?" she grinned the way only Cammie could.

Valerie had to roll her eyes. "Shit, you two are becoming no better than Sandra and Diego."

"Says the lady with commitment problems," Cammie retorted. "I mean, at least I pick a team, even if I play in multiple lanes. You're like that old school game of pong. You're the ball, right... when you going to flip back to the other side?"

Everybody stared at Cammie, completely lost.

"You... have no idea what I'm talking about."

Valerie shook her head. "I got the gist of the insult, if that was an insult, but... pong?"

"Oh, forget it." Cammie rubbed the back of her neck, glancing away, then looked back. "I... actually don't know. I once heard this old guy giving someone that speech, and I had no idea what it meant. So, figured if I use it enough, someday someone will know."

"Cammie, I'm going to miss you."

"Ahhh." Cammie released Royland's hand in favor of a big hug from Valerie. When they were done, Cammie winked and said, "A bit more, to satisfy your curiosity?"

"God!" Valerie said, punching her friend in the shoulder.

Cammie laughed and took a step back, then said to Royland, "Don't try to sexually proposition her, she gets violent."

"Or maybe he'd get what he asked for, just to make you jealous."

Royland took a step back and an intense anger flashed over Cammie's face, but was gone a second later, replaced with a confused, skeptical expression.

"Whoa, kidding," Valerie said, hands up in surrender.

"We can skip the hug," Royland said, even though Cammie was blushing.

"They give you any trouble," Valerie said, "Just kill 'em." She watched the two walk to the side of the ship to join a few of the other pirates, who were staying behind and were loading into the rowboats.

"You know how we do it," Cammie said, and started to climb overboard. "Oh, and for the record, I knew you were joking. And I wasn't jealous."

"Right."

"Okay," Royland said with a laugh.

"What? I wasn't!"

As they laughed, she repeated it a couple more times while disappearing over the side.

"Hey, Cam," Valerie shouted.

"Yeah?" Cammie's voice carried over, losing itself in the wind.

"Tell Bronson and his family, I'll be around."

"You got it."

Valerie stood there, on the deck of this pirate ship-turned-blimp that was now, effectively, hers. It would be weird, not seeing them again for who knows how long. There was too much of that going on lately. Too much saying good-bye to people for the sake of making the world a better place.

But with the things she had been a part of, even if just tangentially, when with the Duke... it was like she owed the world. She damn well meant to see that payment fulfilled. And so it was that, when Robin stepped up next to her, every ounce of her said to pull away, to not open herself up to yet another person who she would only have to, eventually, say good bye to.

Robin seemed to notice, because she paused a foot away, one arm at her side, the other crossed over her chest so that she held herself in a half hug.

"You sure we won't need them?" Robin asked.

Valerie considered the question. "Who knows? An army of pirates, men and women with guns and swords, and then there's the whole slaver thing and who knows how many of them will be on our side. Yeah, I'd say we could use them, but... nothing's been too big to handle so far, so we'll see."

The last of the spare pirates departed, Toiya going with them —she didn't want any more suffering, if possible.

Martha gave the order and the air ship's balloon rose into the air, fully inflated now, and the anti-grav technology kicked in to give them that extra boost.

"You're certain we don't need Bronson or someone to fly this thing?" Valerie asked. "We could still send for him."

Martha headed for the wheel, but paused to say, "This isn't the first ship I've been on. It won't be the last."

Valerie nodded, ready to take a chance on this woman, and

went to the ship's bow to look out to watch the ocean as it would soon disappear from sight. For how long, she had no idea.

With a jolt, the air ship was up and soon moving through the sky, in pursuit of the Pirate Prince. None of that other stuff mattered right now. All of those emotions. No, it was time to kick butt and make the world right again.

CHAPTER SIXTEEN

Outside Old Manhattan

Diego cast a wary glance at the horizon where, although it was still night, hints of dark blue signified the coming sun. With the amount of vampires they had out there with them, this outpost had better show up soon or they'd have to head back, and fast.

"Something crawl up your butt and die?" Platt, one of the vampires from the elevator, asked, giving him a grin.

"He's worried for us," Bryant said, then pulled a black face-mask out of his pack. "Dude, worse comes to worse, here we go. Put these badboys on, ain't no big thing."

"I just don't want to have to explain to my girl why I let so many of you die out here, that's all," Diego said, playing along. It felt good to joke—took the seriousness off the situation. "Not that she'd be worried about you all, just expects better of me."

"Funny boy," Platt said, grinning. "Listen, these jerks out here don't show up soon, I'm going to go looking for some squirrels or something, just to say I killed something."

"Whoa, what'd a squirrel ever do to you?"

Platt pursed his lips, thinking about that. "Fine, no squirrels. Bastards are too cute."

Diego shook his head with a laugh. "How about no killing unless it's necessary?"

"Meh, I guess." Platt licked his lips. "Just been a while since I had a drink."

"You like the taste of blood?"

Platt adjusted the rifle slung over his shoulder. "Like it? I adore it."

Diego glanced over at Bryant, who shrugged and gave him a nod. "You two got issues."

A vampire ran past them in a flash, stopping to speak with Brad and Felix, nodded at their response, and took off back the way she came.

"Scout?" Diego asked, and Bryant nodded.

"We must be close then," Diego said, and was about to excuse himself to go speak with Brad and Felix, when—

KABOOM!

Everything lit up, debris flying in all directions, and an intense heat came over Diego as fire licked his skin. At first, he was simply disoriented, and then a whistling sounded.

"Shit!" he shouted, leaping for cover as the artillery landed near where he'd been standing.

Again with the explosion and debris, and this time accompanied by gunfire.

"Ambush!" someone was shouting, and then Diego saw their mistake—they had been coming up under a ridge, and the enemy must have sent others in a different direction to distract the scouts, while staying out of their enhanced line of sight here.

Men and women screamed as they charged in on the vampires and Weres, and soon, the night was filled with wolves darting among the attackers.

Diego maintained his human form for now and turned, aiming in on a man, but was surprised to see the guy was not only nude but for a loin cloth, but had no weapon. His hair fell over his shoulders and stuck out in a mess, and his eyes were wild.

Instead of shooting him, he brought the butt of his rifle into the man's face, instantly dropping him.

When he looked around, he saw that more attackers were the same as this one, some completely nude, others in ripped jeans. None of them were what you'd expect of real attackers.

Then it hit him—these were just whackos, the crazy people who lived outside of the city walls. Somehow the faction leaders had corralled them into this spot to attack. But they must have known that it wouldn't do any good, a bunch of whackos against Weres and vampires.

So…

"GET OUT OF HERE!" Diego shouted, and began running to get out of what he was sure was the target zone.

There was no question when, a moment later a man appeared in the middle of all the others, explosives strapped to his chest, and he laughed like a hyena in heat before the explosion hit and took out everyone in its radius.

Luckily, most of the Weres and vampires had heard Diego and, while not putting it all together, followed his lead.

But not Bryant, Diego saw. The poor bastard was just a head and torso, crawling toward him.

Could he heal from that? He would probably survive, and if he healed… as just a torso?

Platt stepped forward and, after whispering something in his friend's ear and a quick nod from said friend, he took out his blade and ended it.

When he stood, wiping the blade clean on his own pants, he said, "Where the fuck are they?"

There was no more levity in his voice, no more sparkle in his eye.

Diego thought about saying some B.S. about not wanting to

just go charging in full of rage, but as he stood there, looking at the remains of what had moments ago been a pretty damn cool guy, he could think of nothing other than exacting revenge as well.

Gunshots were still going off, so that was the direction they would go.

"Follow me," he said, and this time, he cast his clothes aside and became the puma. He darted through the night, processing the direction of his companions, closer to the source of the explosion, compared to the attackers on the outer rim.

But he didn't want the ones with the guns—they would be the pawns. He meant to go for the jugular here, and so veered left, his Werecat eyes scanning the night.

There. By a crop of rocks used to block their silhouettes. The fuckers were smart, which gave Diego more satisfaction.

Heavy footsteps told him Platt was coming up fast, and then the vampire was past him, moving in a flash and letting his bullets tear through their opponents.

More flashes of vampires moving in the night, and then the screams started before Diego even reached the enemy.

And then he was among them himself, dodging a pitiful attempt from a guy attacking him with a gardening tool. He spun around and took down his attacker, clawing at his arms and chest, before taking a nice chunk out of his gut. Blood was warm in his mouth, the taste of iron heavy, but in no way liking it as the vampires had described.

All around him was carnage. Not a single one of them left, and then—

Two Weres turned on one of the vampires, then three more had made a move on Platt. They were restraining him to the rock, and the human attackers, more of them, were moving in from hiding spots unseen.

"The hell is this?" Felix shouted beside Diego, having turned back into his human form in all the confusion.

Diego turned back now, too, pulling to the shadows to debate his next move. "Someone's making a move, but who?"

"What side are you on?"

"You have to ask?" Diego stared into Felix's eyes to see if he could trust the man as he thought he could, and the answer he got was yes. "Someone's working with the outsiders, a group of Weres. We stop them, then get to the bottom of this."

"Agreed."

The two transformed again and broke out into the night, making their first priority to free any vampires who had been captured. Anyone still fighting was strong enough that they didn't need to worry about helping, Diego figured.

A burst of flame came from nearby, scorching a large rock and, judging by the screams, a couple of vampires. Flamethrowers—a line of men with them.

Diego didn't want to get caught in that, but couldn't let New York's new army be burned alive. He searched and spotted Sergeant Garcia in a tactical position by the rocks providing cover fire for the vampires. Then he saw Felix, in werewolf form, taking down a woman with a spear and had an idea.

As he ran, he transformed into a human and shouted, "Felix, the spear!"

Felix transformed, tossed him the spear, and then was back as a wolf again for his next attacker. Diego snatched the spear out of the air, spun to jam it through a traitor-Were's throat, and then continued on to use it as he had intended. He ran, crammed it into the hard earth, and then pole-vaulted up and over the rocks. He transformed in the process, pushed off of the rocks for extra momentum and came down hard on the attackers with flamethrowers.

This ambush was well-orchestrated, but that didn't mean it would do a damned thing against the likes of Diego. He was tearing out throats, clawing legs, and taking them down left and right. Felix had seen what was happening and joined in the fight, and they were joined by more and more of the vampires, as they became free.

When the flame-throwers were out of commission, Diego turned back to see a vicious struggle developing between the Weres and vampires. Some Weres had made it to the outskirts of the fight, and Diego guessed by the confusion on their faces and glances in Felix's direction that they weren't in on this scheme.

Which left the rest of them as enemies.

He made a gesture for Felix to stay back, and was glad he didn't have to transform to say so. As he ran forward, he heard Felix shouting for his Weres to rally behind him, and stand by for further word.

Diego was soon in the mix, working his way toward Brad and Platt. They were fighting side by side, outnumbered but certainly not outmatched.

With a roar, Diego was on the closest Were, tearing at the back of his neck and trying to work his way around to the front.

A strike across the Were's jaw from Brad threw it off balance, and then Diego had her—her, he realized, pausing long enough for her to transform into her human form. There before him, was the nude form of Presley.

Diego transformed back, now totally caught off guard. He took a step back, looked around, and then wanted to punch himself as she leaped up and ran.

If she was here, then... He turned, eyes searching for any sign that Esmerelda was in her Were form here as well. Brad and Platt spun like a duo in a perfect dance, and dead Weres fell around them. Felix and his crew had taken out the rest of the human attackers, all but a group that was on the run in the same direction Presley had gone.

But there was no sign of Esmerelda,

Either she was already dead, on the run, or... back in New York. Now that his head was clearing, he was certain she hadn't come. Although, he hadn't thought Presley had come either. Had she dressed herself up like one of the assassin vampires, and somehow he hadn't noticed? Or did she follow and sneak into the attack? He couldn't be sure.

"AFTER THEM!" he shouted, and nobody hesitated to doubt his command.

They hadn't gone far, however, when they saw the point of retreat—a small outpost, what had likely once been a grocery store and had now been barricaded with make-shift fences with spiked poles for defense. Two humans were moving a defensive wall into place, and several Weres were standing just within the fence, ready for the attack in case their pursuers made it in.

Twenty feet from the gate, Diego came to a stop. The rest were with him, Felix and his two remaining Weres on one side, Brad, Platt, and three remaining vampires on the other. Out of the darkness, one more form appeared, his cammies ragged— Sergeant Garcia. No one else. They were the only survivors.

The ambush had done its job.

Diego was too pissed to even consider the fact that he and the Weres had all left their clothes behind. He was finally getting used to that aspect of these wars, though he still preferred to fight with guns when he could, so that it didn't come to this.

"Presley!" he shouted. "What the FUCK?!"

Her face poked out from one of the windows. A vampire lifted a rifle to shoot, but the humans within had rifles aimed back, and two more stepped out with flame throwers.

"I wouldn't try it," Presley said.

"Nobody's shooting anyone until I have an explanation," Diego said. "And know that Sandra's safe."

Presley laughed. "That all depends on where she is, Diego. Is she back home, or is she in the midst of Enforcer HQ? Because if it's the latter…"

Diego felt his chest clench, but he breathed out, trying to focus on the fact that Sandra was likely back in bed, resting right now. But whatever else was happening in the city meant he couldn't relax just yet.

"Mind telling us what exactly is happening?" Brad called out. "Before I rip your head off and mount it on my wall?"

"Since you asked so nicely…" She disappeared from the window and, a moment later, appeared in the doorway with two large rocket launchers, one on each shoulder. "We figured it's time to bring the days of the Were back. We don't answer to humans or vampires, we're Weres, creatures of the night, worthy of worship. They should all bow at our feet and adorn us with gifts."

"And you mean to force them to do so?" Diego shook his head. "When Valerie hears about this…"

"If she does, it'll be too late. This was her fault for putting so much trust in us. How much did she screen us, anyway? Or you for that matter?" She adjusted the rocket launchers. "Last chance, Diego. Show your true colors, cast off these shackles, and join us."

"I'd rather take my chances in hell," he said, and growled mid-transformation, charging forward. The others followed, and the rocket launchers and guns went off.

Earth and fence and body parts exploded and flew through the air, Weres, vampires, and the regular humans collapsed, and then Diego and Presley had connected in a mess of fur and blood, rolling back and forth as their teeth and claws tore into each other's flesh.

Guns continued to go off all around them, but by then, they had bashed in through the door, and she managed to kick him off.

She flipped over, transforming into her human form, and grabbed a pistol. Diego bit into her pistol arm, then tasted hair as she transformed. Teeth sank into the back of his neck, and he thought he was done for. The room spun, and he felt a cold tingling.

Every ounce of him said to surrender to it, that he had lost. To give up. Every ounce, that is, but the one tiny portion of his heart that said Sandra was back in New York, waiting for him, and possibly in trouble.

And not only her—all of the citizens of New York.

With a grunt of pain he transformed into his human form and kicked off of the nearby wall, sending the two of them toppling over the couch and onto the wooden table in the center of the room. They went crashing through it so that it splintered out around them, and they hit the floor with a bang.

Now Diego was free.

One of the wooden legs of the table was within reach, so he lunged. Teeth tore into his calf, pulling him back and he screamed, turning to see the large wolf that was Presley. She released and went for his exposed groin, and he almost screamed in terror, except that his hand had just landed on something hard and metal.

The pistol.

Her teeth inches away from his family jewels, he lifted the pistol and, metal touching her eyeball, pulled the trigger.

Wolf brains splattered everywhere, and continued to as he backed up, shooting over and over until the pistol was emptied and Presley was no more than a pile of bloodied fur.

He was covered in her blood, trying not to gag, as a form appeared in the doorway. Instinctively, Diego lifted the pistol and squeezed—

CLICK.

The bullets were gone, he remembered as he collapsed to his knees.

Strong arms had him, carrying him to a chair, and then he saw Felix before him, eyes wide with concern. Through the ringing in his ears he could barely make out Felix's words as he asked if Diego was okay, and Diego nodded.

"The others?"

JUSTIN SLOAN & MICHAEL ANDERLE

"Only us and Brad left," Felix said, shaking his head. "Brad's injured... He'll need our help, but the sun's coming up."

Diego processed this, then told him about Esmerelda back in New York.

Felix licked his lips, considering this, and then nodded. "I'll protect Brad, watch out to ensure none of those bastards are left out here, then make it back to New York at nightfall. Figure this shit out by then, so I don't have to. I need a break from all this death."

Another form appeared in the doorway and Felix stood, ready for action.

"Put some damn clothes on," Garcia said, the expression in his eyes furious. "A bunch of fucking Weres and vampires think they can kill me? Hell no. I want to see this shit paid for."

"You're coming with me," Diego said, pushing himself up. He was wobbly, blood dripping down the back of his neck, but he could stand and he would heal. Sandra might be in danger, so he was damn sure going to do everything in his power to get to her.

CHAPTER SEVENTEEN

New York, Enforcer HQ

The first gunshots sounded like they were coming from a long way off, distant, as if they were part of Sandra's dream. But when she woke in Valerie's old room, off the old office of Enforcer HQ, now used as a conference room, she heard another shot and knew it was real.

Light was streaming in through the window from the east, the sky blue and peaceful as if everything was right in the world.

Everything except those gun shots.

More sounded, and this time, Sandra bolted out of bed. Her first instinct was to grab her clothes and make for the door. A thought hit her—she wasn't a cop or a soldier, she wasn't a Were or a vampire. In fact, she was pregnant, and had her unborn child to watch out for. That's why she had slept here at Enforcer HQ to begin with. She felt more secure surrounded by friends, especially with Valerie and Diego both gone.

But, of course, nothing was ever safe in this world.

It wasn't like she could just sit by and do nothing anyway, so she went to the hidden opening in the wall that Valerie had showed her, pulled out the shotgun they had stowed there for occasions such as this, a purse full of ammo, and made for the stairs.

Shouting came from below, soldiers moving down the stairs, their voices growing distant.

Yeah, this was stupid. She knew it, but this was her home as much as anyone else's. New York, Enforcer HQ, it was hers to protect. Even if she was a normal, unaltered pregnant lady.

And fuck anyone who tried to take that from her.

She nudged the stairwell door open to take a peek out. When she saw it was clear, she made her way down. The next floor down was quiet, and the next, but then—three stairs away from the landing and the next door—shouting came, followed by a loud explosion that rocked the stairwell and shattered the glass of the door. None of it hit her, but the shock of it made the shotgun shake in her hands—not because she was scared, but because some jerk out there was threatening to put her baby in danger.

With that thought, she threw open the door and charged out into a room of smoke, fallen soldiers, and one person on the far side of the room, opening the door to Commander Donnoly's office.

Esmerelda.

The Were turned to Sandra, sneered, and beckoned to two people to come out. "Get rid of her, then find that bastard. We're not leaving here until he's taken out."

Then she was gone, moving down a side hallway, as two soldiers, a man and a woman, moved toward Sandra. The man had a pistol, already aimed at her, so Sandra ducked around the corner just as drywall exploded where her head had been. A second shot came, blasting a hole in the paneling nearby. Sandra waited, counted to three, and knelt as she spun back around the corner.

As she'd suspected, the cocky ass had advanced, likely not thinking much of this civilian with a shotgun.

So she taught him a lesson, aiming for the legs first. The shots tore through him and he collapsed, screaming. The woman was behind him, rifle ready, but Sandra wasn't so pregnant that she was really slowed down yet. She remembered her training, back in France under the Duke, and rolled, shotgun still aimed, so that when she leveled out, all she had to do was readjust and pull the trigger.

Unfortunately, she missed, and now it was time to reload.

The woman, who had dived out of the way, was standing to aim back in, when Sandra decided that running away would just lead to a chase and be damn scary. So instead, she darted forward, catching the woman with the butt end of the shotgun to her nose. Blood splattered everywhere, and the woman dropped her rifle. A second hit, this time to the temple, sent the woman stumbling backwards.

By the time she processed what had happened and was diving for her rifle, Sandra had already picked it up, tossing the shotgun aside.

"What the hell's happening?" Sandra demanded.

"Go to hell."

"You first," Sandra said, then pulled the trigger. A three-round burst tore through the lady's chest and neck, and she collapsed to the floor.

The man was still there groaning in agonizing pain, and he was reaching for a pistol holstered on his belt.

Sandra stomped on his hand and then aimed in at his head. "Talk."

He grunted, clenched his teeth, and just stared. So she shot his arm.

"DAMMIT!" he shouted, struggling to move, but she kicked him in the face.

"Listen here, jackass. I'm pregnant and trying to get my beauty sleep. What I don't need is your B.S." More shots sounded, muffled, followed by another explosion. "So talk now, or see what happens when you wake a pregnant woman from her sleep."

He clenched his jaw, trying to fight the pain, and said, "The Weres, they've promised some of us power, freedom from the old ways."

"You're an idiot," she said, then shot him in the forehead. Then to herself, she added, "This city isn't for the taking."

With that, she followed the hallway that Esmerelda had taken, rifle at the ready. She paused at the corner and checked the magazine. Still full, minus about five shots. Not bad.

She lifted it, keeping it close, and aimed in as she peeked around the corner. Clear. Moving briskly, she ran forward. She didn't have much of a plan other than shoot anyone trying to shoot her, and stopping Esmerelda.

That would have to do for now.

A man lay groaning on the floor at the next hall, near the door to the bathroom. Sandra was about to check on him when a large, hairy form crossed into the hallway ahead.

It suddenly hit Sandra that she wasn't just a woman in a building full of possible assailants, but she was hunting a werewolf. Not her finest hour.

"Get out of here!" the man yelled, pulling a pistol from an ankle holster and rolling in his own blood so that he could aim in at the werewolf.

Sandra ducked into the bathroom door, just far enough to get cover, and then aimed in, joining the man in plugging the werewolf full of holes.

The beast fell back, staggering. The man's pistol clicked, the chamber back—out of bullets.

But that didn't matter—they had the beast.

Or so she thought.

It suddenly lunged forward, taking the man by the neck and tossing him from side to side like a squeaky toy, while Sandra tried to get a clean shot.

After a few seconds of this, she realized it didn't matter if she got a clean shot or not—if anything, it was now better to hit the guy and put him out of his suffering. So instead of staying there and taking any chances, she darted out of hiding and ran forward, unloading the magazine along the way. Bullets tore into man and werewolf alike.

When she stopped, the bullets spent, the man lay limp, his eyes staring up, lifeless. The wolf was shuddering. She might heal, but not if Sandra acted quickly.

She lifted the rifle to smash in the beast's head and paused. Not a she, she realized as the wolf turned back to a man, his junk fully exposed.

"Where is she?" Sandra demanded. "Where's Esmerelda?"

"Please…" he said, hands up in defense. But the look in his eyes wasn't terror, it was humor. "Please look behind you."

She couldn't think of any last words that would put more terror into her heart right now, especially as she noted the two shadows moving.

Then the growl came.

Not even bothering to spin and look, she ran for the opposite wall where another doorway was, kicked in, and then threw it shut with all her weight against it as two werewolves slammed into it from the other side with a loud thud. It was the women's bathroom. Good thing boys weren't allowed, she thought to herself with a crazed chuckle.

Where the hell had those two come from?

Brain spinning, breaths coming in short bursts, she tried to find her calm as the door continued to thud. She clicked the door's lock shut, but knew that wouldn't keep them long. She pushed her back against the door, eyes darting for any way out of there, and then, just as she had spotted the side-door that must lead to another hallway, a whimper came from one of the stalls.

A young recruit to the force peered out of the stall, saw her, then closed the stall door with a slam.

"You're on my side, yeah?" Sandra shouted to the woman over the thuds of the doors behind her.

"I'm damn sure not on theirs." The woman's voice cracked, but she peeked back out through the door. "What's happening?"

"A coup, it'd seem." Sandra shuddered as the door shook so bad she was sure it was about to fall from its hinges.

And then it was silent.

She waited, listening to distant gunshots and two explosions, then looked up to make eye contact with the woman.

Instead of talking, she motioned to the other door, and raised her eyebrows in a way that asked if she got it.

The woman nodded, then reached to her side and drew her pistol. Taking it in both hands, she moved for the other door, then waited.

Sandra breathed, counted to three, and then made her way over there. She slowly opened the door, the woman with the pistol at her side, and checked. Clear.

"You got a name?" Sandra whispered.

"Bertie," she said, then gave Sandra a look as if she was going to say something about the name.

"Stick close," Sandra said, then motioned to the empty chamber of the rifle. "I'm all out... oh, and name's Sandra."

Bertie nodded, forced a smile, and then followed Sandra out into the hallway. Once they were clear, they started running, and just in time, too—a moment later, an explosion sounded from behind, followed by the banging of what Sandra guessed was the bathroom door flying off its hinges. She glanced back to see smoke coming out from under the door they'd just come through, and then pulled Bertie out of the main hallway and through a doorway, just as the sound of that door being flung open sounded.

She spun, looking for a way out, and was flabbergasted to see that they were back in Colonel Donnoly's office!

It wasn't a large office, not compared to the one Valerie had occupied, anyway. But it was practical—a desk, some paintings, and a sword on the wall. Sandra smiled at that. Back in the days before New York, the sword had been her specialty. Specifically, this kind—a katana.

Yes, she got that others thought the large claymore type of sword was more practical, or even the rapiers and cutlasses the pirates used. But she thought that was only true if you lacked grace and style.

She pulled the sword from the wall, tested it with her eyes on the door they'd just come through, and then realized she was rubbing her belly subconsciously. Bertie was watching, curiously, and Sandra gave her a brief nod before saying, "Hide."

The wolves were outside, sniffing and growling. There was no doubt they'd find them.

The only option was to stand their ground and be as ready as they could ever be.

From the other side of the door, the sounds grew louder, and Bertie made a scraping sound as she bumped into the desk, trying to hide behind it. Sandra cringed, sword at the ready, waiting for that door to come bursting forward any moment.

A gunshot.

Not from in here, but the hallway, then shouting and more shooting.

The two women shared a look, both amazed at their luck. Sandra ran to the door, pressed her ear against, it, and then said, "I'm going out there."

"Are you insane?"

Sandra debated, then nodded. "You know, that might explain it. Yeah, I think I'm insane. Wanna join me, or…?"

Bertie just stared at her, mouth hanging open, then licked her lips. "Fuck it."

"Fuck it?"

"Yeah," Bertie smiled, held her pistol up at the ready, "Fuck it."

Sandra smiled, and then threw open the door to see that, several soldiers were shooting from the elevators as the two werewolves made their way through the shots to the attack.

If she didn't act, the bullets might not be enough to stop those werewolves. But if she ran into the fray, she might get shot. Unlike them, she didn't heal. And she couldn't risk that, for the baby's sake.

"Distract them," Sandra said.

"What?"

"Shoot them, get their attention back on us. Or, at least one of them. I have a plan."

Bertie looked dubious, but she shrugged, held the pistol, and squeezed the trigger. The shot was loud and left a ringing in Sandra's ears that she was going to regret, but for now, it had its effect.

The werewolf she'd hit spun on them, eyes curious, saliva dripping from its exposed teeth. The scent of gunpowder filled the hallway. The roaring of the werewolf was almost louder than the shots going off.

Sandra stepped back and said, "Move against the wall. Hit it again as soon as it enters the doorway."

Bertie did as she was told, but when the werewolf came charging through, leaping and pushing off of the doorway, neither could have been prepared for its trajectory. That didn't stop Sandra from acting, though. With a quick motion, she practiced the thrust she had perfected in France.

Straight forward, the blade slid through the werewolf's neck. The momentum of the beast carried Sandra with it and then pulled the sword from her hands. When she recovered, she saw the werewolf on the floor, struggling to stand.

Bertie shot it once in the eye, and it shuddered with a spasm. Then Sandra ran up, grabbed the sword's handle, and slammed her foot down on the back of the blade so that it sliced through the rest of the neck, doing a nice job of half-decapitating the werewolf.

The blade snapped in half as she pulled it free, but the jerk was dead.

Cheers rose out from the hallway, and a moment later two men appeared in the doorway, ready to shoot.

"Whoa, whoa!" Sandra said, dropping the sword. "Good guys here!"

It took her a moment to realize that one of them was Colonel Donnoly, the other Sergeant Davies.

"The wolf?" she asked.

"Thanks to you dealing with this one," Davies said with a nod of approval, "we were able to focus our efforts and deal with it."

"Esmerelda?"

Donnoly shook his head. "We haven't found her. We don't know how many of the Weres are part of this, so we're rounding them up."

"All of them?"

"You think we have a choice?" Davies asked. "The truth is we don't know who she's working with."

"That's wrong," Sandra said. "You know it is, or you wouldn't be looking at me like that right now."

Donnoly took her in for a moment, then seemed to make up his mind. "You shouldn't be here. You need to think of the baby."

"I also need to think of the city, or the baby won't have a future," she said. "In case you don't remember, I just saved our asses."

"We all just saved our asses," he said. "While Esmeralda's at large, you should be in safe-keeping. Davies, take her to Valerie's old office and see that she has a guard."

"To protect me or to protect you?" Sandra spat out.

"Is that a threat?"

She stepped toward him. "Diego's a Were. He's the father of my baby. That means you're threatening to hold the father of my baby accountable for all this, to lock him up? If that's true, then you bet your ass I'm threatening you."

Donnoly glared, then said, "Davies, I gave an order."

Sandra looked between him and Davies, then to Bertie, and said, "I know the way."

She started walking, ignoring the fact that Davies was following, two men with him. It didn't surprise her that Donnoly wouldn't let Bertie be one of her guards. Bertie and Davies she could persuade to help her, she imagined. Not two strangers.

As the elevator doors closed behind them, Sandra noted the silence, how the shots and explosions had stopped.

But her mind was reeling with the thought of what was coming next. Esmerelda could attack again at any minute, and maybe had more Weres or regular fighters still on her side.

Even if she was out of the picture, the way Donnoly was talking only meant more infighting, more animosity. She'd have to make sure she was out of here as soon as possible, so that she could do her part.

CHAPTER EIGHTEEN

Flying Across Canada

Valerie stood at the helm of the air ship, holding onto the railing and looking out at the blimps ahead of them. Her ship was keeping its distance, under the guidance of Martha, relying on Valerie and Robin's eyesight to keep them on track. Since they could both see better than non-enhanced humans, they had figured this out as a way of following without being detected.

The only downside would be if the other blimps had vampires on board. There wasn't any reason to suspect so, except for the fact that Kaine had been traveling with them.

Whether there were vampires aboard or not, the air ships hadn't slowed or turned back to fire at Valerie's ship. So far, so good.

Robin had chosen to retreat below deck rather than have to wear her assassin protective gear during the day time. That left Valerie with Martha and River, as the rest of the pirates were either sailing the ship or resting for their next shift.

The early sunrise hit canyons below, tall trees nearly scraping the base of the ship. Valerie hadn't even known that trees could grow like that, or that so much green still existed in the world.

"Why don't you go inside," River said, coming out to join her. "We have their course, at least for a bit. "Get some rest."

Valerie considered this. She definitely could use some shut-eye.

"Come on," he said, "Robin's already up anyway. She said she can keep watch from the control room."

"And what would I do with myself as I lay there trying to sleep?" Valerie asked. "The thoughts of what's happening back in New York, or to Robin's family... I can't imagine sleeping right now, no matter how badly I need it."

She stood staring out at the blimps, watching the hills in the distance, and then nodded. "I'll... take a break."

While sleep was likely impossible at the moment, if Robin was up, she wanted to speak with her. Making her way to the control deck, Valerie glanced up at the morning sky, contemplating everything going on up there.

If she partnered with TH, went up to space with him, would she really join the legendary vampire, the Queen Bitch herself? That title still made her laugh. What nearly omnipotent leader went by a title like that? Must be one with a good sense of humor, that was for sure.

When that day came, she felt she would be ready for it. Something about the world... she was doing her best to change it, but wondered if she just didn't really fit.

The door to the control room opened and Martha stepped out, rubbing her eyes. She smiled and nodded, then said, "I'm going below deck to rest. Giving the controls to Robin for a bit."

"Robin?"

"It's basically on autopilot, but she wanted to give it a go."

Valerie nodded, impressed, and smiled at Martha as she walked off. Entering the control room, Valerie noted how this one was larger than the blimp Captain Bronson had taken them in. It had weapons lining the walls, guns and swords, and even an oversized pirate captain's hat hanging from a wall hook.

"Not putting on the hat?" Valerie teased Robin, who she saw now at the control panel. The woman had a hand on the wheel, and turned back with a frown.

"These are the same jackasses who took my parents into slavery. I don't think I'll be dressing up like them any more than I have to."

"Shit, sorry." Valerie came over and stood next to Robin, looking out through the rosy window with her. "I didn't mean anything by it."

Robin nodded. "No, I know." After a moment of silence, she added, "And I didn't mean to bite your head off. It's just... this could be it. We might be damn close, and it feels surreal."

"When it comes to it, I mean, just save them and get out of here, you know?"

Robin shook her head. "I don't know. What do you mean?"

"You might blame all of those so-called pirates, for what happened."

"Because they did it," Robin said, voice growing harsh. "Of course I blame them."

"Yes, but..." Valerie breathed deep, trying to think about how to say it. "Maybe focus on stopping it, you know? The revenge part of it can cloud your judgment, make you do things you'll spend the rest of your life regretting. You're not a murderer, I know you."

"Would've been nice to tell that to the bastards who took me from my family and turned me into this monster that I am now."

"You think you're a monster?" Valerie felt her gut clench at that, as if she'd been punched.

Robin realized what she had implied there and said, "Oh, no, I don't mean that you're a monster. It's just that..."

"Robin, you're only a monster if you let them turn you into one. Save your family, save all the slaves. But don't succumb to the darkness."

Silence followed, then Robin muttered something about trying, but it didn't sound very committed.

Valerie understood, to a degree. She had been obsessed with revenge after her brother nearly left her for dead. No matter how much she convinced herself that it was about justice back then, she now saw it for what it really was. It could easily have consumed her to the point of no return.

Luckily for her, she had friends around to keep her straight. Well, maybe not straight, exactly, but they acted as anchors in the storm, that was for sure.

Not knowing what to do here, Valerie reached out to put her hand on Robin's, but Robin just moved hers, so that Valerie grabbed hold of the steering wheel. For a moment, she held it as if that had been on purpose, but then she let go and turned to leave.

"Val," Robin said, voice full of excitement.

Valerie turned around, curious, and saw that Robin had both hands on the wheel, staring out the window intently.

"The blimps," Robin said, "they've begun their descent."

Valerie went back to the window and squinted, smiling to see that, sure enough, it was beginning. All this other B.S. could be tossed aside for now, because it was go time.

"Martha went to rest," Valerie said. "Think you could bring the ship down by yourself?"

Robin smiled, biting her lip. "I think I'll give it a go."

"Just… don't kill us."

With a laugh, Robin brought the air ship around to the right, circling first so that they gave the others enough room to land while still keeping their own ship out of sight.

"There," Valerie said, pointing to some hills just north of them, where it was clear that there was a line of black shapes that must have been buildings. "We can land on the other side of those hills, unnoticed, and then make our way over undetected."

"Roger that," Robin said, and began to steer the ship in that direction. She seemed almost giddy, as if all of their discussions had been forgotten, as if she were about to go to relax along the beaches of France, not storm into a pirate stronghold to set a bunch of slaves free.

And that attitude worried Valerie more than if Robin had been frowning or crying.

"What's going on?" River asked when he came back in. Soon, several of the others had joined them, including Martha.

Valerie explained, and Martha sat back with her arms folded, watching Robin.

"You're letting her land the ship?" River asked. "You never let me!"

"She's a grown woman," Martha said. "And I'm curious." She glanced over at him and smiled. "She does well, I'll let you do the next one."

He leapt forward to Robin's side and started telling her about different buttons that slowed the airflow and made turns sharper, suddenly eager to ensure she succeeded, and Robin was loving it.

"What exactly are we getting ourselves into here?" Valerie asked Martha, while the others were distracted.

"Far as I know," Martha replied, "this'll be one of several outposts. There's no telling if her family will be here, but I can guarantee it'll be one of the larger outposts."

"Why's that?"

"The Prince wouldn't be stopping here if it wasn't. He's either gathering reinforcements, or warning the eight leaders."

"Now you're telling me there's like, what, a consortium of pirate leaders or some such crap?"

Martha chuckled. "To be fair, not all of us refer to ourselves as pirates. It's just a thing most of us along the coast started adapting after others put the label on us. A lot of the groups don't even pirate, but… it got worse with Kaine around. There was no one to resist him, so it kept going."

"And now, under Cammie and Royland?"

"I think this world is coming around," Martha said. "There's going to be friction along the way, that's for sure. But any kind of energy requires friction, doesn't it?"

"And we're moving in the right path," Valerie said with a nod. "It's not every day you get to be part of setting the world back on the right path."

Martha shook her head. "I can honestly say I never thought that'd be in my stars."

"We move in, keep a low profile, and make our move when we have the lay of the land," Valerie said. "When we know who the violent actors are, those aligned most closely with the Prince."

"Exactly... That is, if that's something you all are capable of."

"We deserve that," Valerie said, thinking back on how fast their undercover operation to get close to the Prince had fallen apart. "But it'll be different this time."

"How so?"

"We're committed. There're more lives at stake... I don't know. Those sound like good reasons to me."

Martha nodded. "Me too, but remember that reason doesn't always hold when emotions are in play."

"Who made you Ms. Wise all of a sudden?"

"My nephew would say it's more like Ms. Pain-in-the-butt, but thank you."

Valerie nodded, then found a corner of the ship where she could watch the ground approaching. She wanted a moment of silence to prepare for what was coming and to reassess everything going on. Robin was in a different place than her, what with trying to rescue her family. She got that, and realized it was better to just be there for her right now, to help her through this. Maybe then they could talk about silly things like feelings.

Right now, Valerie needed to ensure she had the sharpest swords possible, loaded pistols, and a scowl that looked the part of a pirate.

CHAPTER NINETEEN

Old Manhattan

The city looked dark and gloomy this day, in spite of the sun sparkling off of the tall buildings. Diego and Garcia took the long route to Enforcer HQ, both keeping their eyes peeled for any sign of violence.

All was silent. There wasn't a single gunshot or explosion, but it was also one of those mornings where all the homeless were off the streets. It was eerie, like they were walking into a city that no one had lived in for years.

"You all out west deal with shit like this?" Diego asked.

Garcia chuckled. "Everyone has their problems. Lucky for those under TH, he doesn't let anything slide. He keeps a tight fist, if you know what I mean."

"It's a strange saying, but sure, I gotcha." He heard a sound and thought a shadow moved in the nearby alley, but after a second, nothing happened, so he moved on. "This is why I left Spain, honestly."

"I thought I detected an accent, but, you know…"

"I'm Asian, so you didn't want to ask?"

Diego nodded. "It's a long story, but yeah. Mostly grew up on the streets. Lucky for me, fending for yourself as a Were isn't all that tough. Even for a kid."

"Damn... Sorry to hear it. I mean, it must've been harsh, though."

Diego shrugged. "In many ways, yeah. That's why I'm such a softy when it comes to Sandra and having a kid on the way. I want to be the father I never had, you know? The husband she needs, so that my kid and my wife never have to experience that loneliness. Don't you dare crack a joke about me being less manly for it either, or I'll crack your skull."

"The thought didn't cross my mind," Garcia said with a chuckle. "You two are married, then?" Garcia glanced over, curious. "When I said something about it before, I coulda sworn there was this confusion in her eyes."

"Does it matter? Out here, is there such a thing as a true husband and wife anymore? Yeah, sure, the village elder, clan leader, or mayor or whatever the hell authority figure there is might make it official, but I don't see that as any more official than what we've got."

"A man of wisdom," Garcia said.

He paused, held up a hand, and gestured to the street ahead. Sure enough, something moved there, then was gone.

Diego was about to give chase, when a pod rounded the corner on the opposite side, then two more. They hovered nearby, then all three opened their doors to reveal soldiers with rifles aimed in on Diego.

"The hell's this?" he asked, hands up. "The coup won then, I take it?"

"Drop your weapons to the ground," a voice called out from the middle one. "The Were's coming with us, into custody."

Diego pursed his lips, considering this. "And if I say no?"

"Sir, do as commanded or we will use force."

He glanced at Garcia to see if he could get a read on what the man was thinking, and Garcia nodded. What choice did they have?

Unslinging his rifle, Diego held it out to show he was lowering it, when out from the left, where they had spotted the other shape, a whooshing sounded, followed by a trail of smoke and then—

CABOOM!

The first pod exploded, hit by what must have been a rocket launcher. It slammed into the next one over, but the third one pulled out of their path, turning to open fire on whoever was in the alley.

"Go!" Garcia said, pulling Diego back so they could run the other way.

Two more forms appeared from the window overhead, shooting up the pod behind Diego and Garcia as they escaped.

"What the hell's wrong with you New Yorkers?" Garcia shouted, ducking down another alley and leading them in the general direction of Enforcer HQ.

"Not enough outlets for our aggression, I assume," Diego replied, ducking under a partially lowered fire-escape. "Thing is, it never seems to let up long enough for me to catch my breath."

"Well, that's something we'll have to put a stop to, isn't it?"

"Damn right."

They came to a stop as four soldiers came at them, former Enforcers now wearing the uniform Donnoly had started to institute—black with a patch over the left shoulder that had the symbol of a sword over a golden circle on it.

"On the ground!" one of the soldiers shouted, but then a smoke grenade rolled in, stopping at their feet. It exploded with a blast that left the smoke to fill their lungs and leave them hacking, and then a figure ran through, shouting for Diego and Garcia to follow.

Two streets over, the figure turned and Diego stopped when he saw who it was.

JUSTIN SLOAN & MICHAEL ANDERLE

"Esmerelda."

"You want to be their prisoner?" she asked. "If not, get your ass moving."

Garcia aimed in at her with his rifle. "This is the bitch whose buddy tried to kill us?"

"Tried to...?" Esmerelda held up her hands, looking baffled. "No, not Presley. Right? I mean, if she did anything to hurt you, I had no idea."

"What's going on here, then?" Diego asked, pulling his own rifle up now, too.

"Both of you calm the hell down," Esmerelda said. "They're making a move against us, the humans. They want all Weres and vampires out of the picture. We can't just sit by and let that happen."

Diego shook his head. "I would agree with you, if I believed that was the case. But Presley already spilled the beans. So, we've got a problem."

"Yes, we do," she said, gesturing for them to look around. When they did, they weren't surprised to see several Weres and soldiers with guns aimed in on them.

"We've faced worse," Garcia said, smiling.

"You won't walk out of this one," Esmerelda said. "Last chance."

"Yeah, just give me a sec," Diego said, glancing in Garcia's direction. Garcia got the message and ducked into a backwards roll as Diego transformed and leapt out of the way of the gunfire that opened up on the spot they'd been standing.

Esmerelda started swearing, then tore off her clothes as she transformed and gave chase to Diego. He'd have to hope Garcia could fend for himself, because he was half the size of Esmerelda transformed, and right now needed to get the hell out of there if they hoped to escape and survive.

He dove into the first window he found open, then made it across a work bench and past a line of furniture left half-assembled, then darted up a stairway as a crash sounded below.

He transformed long enough to open the closest door, then closed it behind him before transforming again to dart across another room, this one littered with raw lumber. He made it to the window and considered jumping, but then reconsidered.

Glancing around, he came up with a plan. He became a human and ran over to the corner where he found a sledge-hammer and a nail gun among the other tools.

Sweet.

Then he ran over and knelt by the door.

As soon as it burst open, he was ready with the nail gun. First, he sent a nail into Esmerelda's leg to surprise her, then one into her foot to keep her in place. It went right through and into the floor, as he'd hoped.

She was in her human form from having to open the door, but now transformed again. It was instantaneous, but he had been planning on that, too, and had already stood and brought the hammer up… and down.

THWONK.

She collapsed, out cold, with the strike of that sledge hammer to her head. Hell, for all he knew, she might be dead and, frankly, he didn't give a damn.

He pulled her foot up so that the nail went right through, and cringed. If she was still alive, that was going to hurt like a bitch when she awoke. That's what she got for trying to kill him and take over the city.

She was heavy like this, but he managed to get her over his shoulders and carry her down the stairs, glad to see they weren't far from Enforcer HQ now. He began the trudge over.

It was only when he saw the grin on the face of a bloodied Garcia that he realized how ridiculous he must look. A completely nude man, covered in blood, carrying a wolf over his shoulders as if it was a decorative fashion piece.

"You, uh, lost your clothes," Garcia said, tossing them over.

"Hold on." Diego tossed Esmerelda in wolf form to the ground, almost enjoying the thud she made against the cement, and then started dressing. "You took out all those guys by yourself, then went back for my clothes?"

"Hey, I couldn't have you walking around making the rest of us look bad."

"Is that… a dick joke?" Diego scoffed. "I don't know why, but I thought you TH army guys were too, I don't know, mature for that."

"Maybe you all are rubbing off on me."

"As long as we're not rubbing one off on you."

Garcia frowned.

"Too far?" Diego asked.

"I just don't know the saying. Should I be offended, or amused?"

"Amused… but I'm not explaining it."

Garcia laughed. "Well, then I'm offended. But don't worry, I'll figure out a way to get you back."

"I don't doubt it," Diego said, finally dressed. He noticed three soldiers emerging from Enforcer HQ, rifles aimed out, Davies among them. "Hey, you all misplace this one?"

He gestured to Esmerelda, and one of them ran back, likely for support, while Davies and the other jogged over.

"You took her out?" Davies asked, inspecting her. "She's still alive, but… what's this? You put a nail through her paw?"

"It was a foot at the time," Diego said. "But… yeah."

"Damn. Whatever it takes, right?" Davies shook his hand. "We owe you one."

"What you owe me is telling me where Sandra is."

Davies' face went pale.

"Where the fuck is my wife, Davies?"

"We… kinda have her on lockdown. In Valerie's old office."

Diego shook his head and started walking into the building.

"You take care of the wolf. You might want to warn your guys, if anyone tries to stop me or continue to detain Sandra, they're going flying from a window. Probably one of the top ones."

"I'd listen to him," Garcia said. "It's been a tough night."

Diego was glad to see Garcia join him a moment later. The soldier who had been with Davies went running past them with a worried glance their way, and Diego paused to let him take the first elevator.

"Might want to give them a second, so we don't have to kill anyone," Garcia said.

"Yeah, might." Diego had lost his sense of humor when hearing that they'd effectively locked up Sandra. But he had guessed what had happened, after those soldiers tried to take him into custody. He was going to have a long talk with Donnoly.

Finally, the second elevator opened and they rode it up to the old office. When they exited, three soldiers stood there with Donnoly, and Sandra, arms folded across her chest.

Diego was about to say something to Donnoly, when he noticed the red hand print on his face.

"You already had a talk with him?" he asked his wife.

She nodded, too pissed to smile, but then her joy at seeing him won over and she ran to give him a big kiss.

"This city's going to take some work," Garcia said, glaring at Donnoly.

"Good thing you're here to help us," Diego said, with a nod of thanks to Garcia. "And good thing Donnoly here's man enough to let smarter people than him make decisions. Isn't that right?"

Donnoly grunted something, but nodded.

"Good," Garcia said, standing tall. "First things first, we're going to set up an internal defense system here, so this can never happen again. Then, starting tomorrow because I need some sleep first, I'll start training the troops. You can be damn sure that I'm going to be testing their loyalty along the way." He turned to Donnoly, head cocked. "I know you're doing what you think's best, and I'm not here to tell you how to run your city. But I damn sure hope we can work together. What'ya say?"

Donnoly looked defeated, lost. But these words made him perk up slightly, and he nodded. "Yes, I'd like that."

"Good. Send out word to your men that the bad wolves and their followers have fallen, along with those out in the field. It's rebuilding time."

Diego held out his arm and then Sandra looped her arm through his. "Come, m'lady. This sir needs a nap."

"Judging by the way you're talking, a long one," she said with a chuckle.

He smiled, glad to be home and to feel her at his side.

CHAPTER TWENTY

Slaver's Peak

Slaver's Peak didn't look as well-kept as last time the Prince had been here for fighters. The pickings must've grown slim, or Captain Greenhand had grown weak.

He'd see to it that all of that changed, once he reached Toro and told the council about this. They understood power like he did, they saw the need for a steady stream of new cut-throats.

He strode forward, leaving the three airships behind as he headed for the main tent. The sun was strong overhead, but he wore his red hat, a broad-rimmed captain's hat that gave him shade. They would see him coming by the way the sunlight glinted off of the gold trim on his hat and long coat, a fact that he enjoyed. Anytime royalty entered a room, the underlings should be ready. As far as he was concerned, everyone but the council in Toro was his underling.

The others at his side were shorter than he was, but hand-picked. His best fighters, his most loyal subjects.

When they reached the tent, two of his men pulled the tent flaps apart. Jessabel led the way to announce his coming. As much as he disregarded her and, at the moment despised her, he had to admit that she was his best with a blade. The other two were excellent marksmen when it came to rifles and rail guns.

"On your feet, you mangy dogs," Jessabel shouted. "The Prince adorns you with his presence."

"Don't come in here with that shit," a stout man said, stepping forward and waving for his men to stay seated or keep on with what they were doing. He wore a baseball cap and had the look of a special forces soldier, ignoring the gray beard.

Jessabel pulled her blade on him, but the Prince held up a hand.

"And who are you?" the Prince asked.

"They call me Apex," the man said. "I took over for Green-hand. Appointed by the Pirate Council, on account of this place going to shit under his command."

The Prince chewed at the inside of his cheek as he considered this, then nodded for Jessabel to stand down.

"You've heard of me?" he asked.

Apex nodded. "Kind words have been said about your skills, less kind words about your sanity."

Jessabel and the others glared, but the Prince simply broke out in laughter.

"Good, good," he said. "Then my hard work has been paying off. I've come to collect. I need fighters."

Apex nodded, but held out his hands. "Apex requires payment. More than before."

"More?"

"Double."

At this, the Prince was about to argue, but his gut clenched and he turned, arms shaking.

"What is it?" Jessabel asked.

"No time for this haggling bullshit," the Prince replied. "She's here, I feel it. Le Diable. She's found us… she's come to claim my soul."

"Fucker's crazy as they say," Apex said to one of his men.

But the Prince wasn't listening. Instead, he was stepping back into the shadows, eyes searching, debating how best to bring this fight to the she-devil. Because he was sure his feeling was right. He didn't know how she had found him, but she had.

He continued to retreat to the shadows, deeper and deeper, until he found a doorway to the back room. Before disappearing through it, he turned, pointing at Apex, and said, "Bring me her fucking head, or I'll have your balls on a platter."

The last thing he heard before ducking out of sight was a comment by Apex, once again confirming his opinion the Prince was a fucking lunatic. Well that was just fine by him, because the next time he saw Apex, the man would have this vampire bitch's head rolling across the floor like a soccer ball, or would be dead himself. The Prince motioned to his followers and warned them to get him armed and ready, just in case, though he sure hoped he wouldn't have to get his hands dirty.

Even the birds were too exhausted by the heat to chirp in the sweltering mid-afternoon sun. Valerie couldn't imagine how horrible it must've been for Robin under her old assassin clothes.

"It wasn't so bad up there," River said. "What gives?"

"Up there we were at a higher altitude and had the wind," Martha replied.

They left the other pirates behind to guard the ship and be ready for a quick getaway, figuring infiltrating with a small group would be better. So, just the four of them—Valerie, Robin, Martha, and River were walking along the dirt path that traversed the hill.

"What the hell could they have slaves working on out here anyway?" Valerie asked.

"It's not about working on stuff," Martha said. "It's about uncovering something."

"You're going to keep it so cryptic?"

Martha laughed. "Honestly, it's not like I know what they're after either. But I've heard rumors. Like that there was a place up here, hidden out where people didn't go in the days before the Great Collapse. Back then, it was cold. People had no reason to explore this far in the cold. But there's one among the pirates who claims there used to be something out here, something like your Area 51."

"And they're trying to find it?"

River beamed, happy to answer this one. "They already did, supposedly."

"And...?"

Martha shook her head. "That's where our knowledge stops. I don't think anyone knows what they've found down there, other than the ones who did the finding."

"If they found anything at all," River interjected.

"My nephew, the skeptic," Martha sad.

"I'm just saying, I've heard multiple stories. One is that they're building some big weapon, or a cache of weapons, with the idea that they'll set up an army and be ready to take over."

"Take over what?" Robin asked.

"Everything."

Valerie frowned and was about to say that didn't seem likely, not with the numbers she had seen, but Robin spoke first.

"That fits with what was happening with the Black Plague. They had us training to be killers, and I wondered where all the weapons came from."

"So... No aliens?" Martha said with a frown.

"There are definitely aliens," Valerie answered. "But that doesn't mean there's necessarily an Area 51 style place around here."

Coming around the hill, they found the sandy valley that led to a series of tents and several buildings, along with lines of people training.

"Looks like the formation of an army isn't so far-fetched," Valerie said.

"This is all too familiar." Robin knelt beside Valerie, hands clenched into fists. "But if they're slaves, like I was, forced to do this against their will, they aren't the enemy."

"So... your idea about fitting in?" Valerie asked, turning to Martha. "With what group?"

Martha looked flustered, but then pointed past the groups to more tents, practically camouflaged against the brown of it all.

"There," she said. "We won't last long if everyone knows each other, or the Prince spots us, knowing who we'd be... as the only outsiders. But that's where I'd bet they'll be."

"Then that's where we go," Valerie replied. "But if this turns into yet another blood bath, I'm going to be pissed."

"How could it not?" Robin replied.

Valerie just sighed. "Well, let's get it over with then."

She stood and started walking. A moment later, Robin hissed and pulled her back.

"Are you forgetting something?" Robin asked. "I can't just walk up there like this!"

"Actually," Valerie looked her up and down, an idea dawning on her. "They probably haven't heard about what happened to the Black Plague. How would they have?"

"You can't be serious."

"What?" River asked as he and Martha caught up. "Be serious about what?"

"She wants me to walk in there like this and pretend I'm here representing the group that enslaved me. But what I don't get, is what that will accomplish."

"You say you were attacked, that you're here for more fighters," Valerie replied.

"They aren't vampires."

187

"You'll make them into vampires. Well, not really, but that's what we say."

"And then…?"

"By then, we'll have seen what we're dealing with, and be ready to make a move."

Robin shook her head, but then said, "Fine," and continued walking on.

"There you go," Valerie said with a smile, and followed.

All four walked right past a group of fighters training with swords. The closest group paused to look at them, but seeing Robin in her all black, they quickly turned back to their training. It seemed she wasn't the first of her type that they had come across.

Valerie held her head strong, telling herself not to lose her cool or give anything away. Two men with rifles stood outside of the largest tent, so that's the one she went to, walking straight up to them, and passing through into the tent.

Not the best guards, she thought with a smirk.

The tent was filled with men and woman in various pirate attire, some in dismal black covering all but their faces, others with extravagant hats and others still with bright reds and yellows.

It was almost laughable, Valerie thought, if it weren't for the fact that they were all killers.

Not a one looked up, or not until she approached the nearest group and said, "We need to speak with the Prince."

The pirate glared at her, a darker man with a shaved head and tattoos on his arms. He nodded toward Robin and said, "You with her?"

"That's right."

"Then you need to see Apex before you see the Prince."

"Yes, Apex," Valerie replied, trying not to laugh at that name.

The man stared at her, then scoffed. "You must be new. He

turned and pointed to a man at the far end of the room. He wore a baseball cap, dark shades even though they were in the tent, and had a gray beard. His T-shirt was tucked into a pair of cargo pants.

"Of course," Valerie said, feeling her story falling apart already. She started walking over, hoping the others were close behind. One man looked up at her and started to stand, and she sensed his aura of violence, so she gave out the slightest bit of fear. It was enough to sit him back down, and she smiled at the look of confusion in his eyes.

Only, a funny thing happened by the time she had reached Apex. For one, she decided that she wasn't here to play games. Not a single one of these jackholes stood a chance against her, physically. All that mattered was the safety of those slaves, and seeing their release.

So, when she stepped up to Apex, she had already decided that the charade was off.

"I'm Valerie, the liberator of New York. The Dark Messiah's Justice Enforcer." She stood tall before him, each hand on a hilt of her swords. "You're going to let the slaves go."

Apex turned to look at her and she saw herself in the reflection of his shades. He also saw her companions behind her, staring in shock. His aura came across like a chilled drink, refreshing but slightly off-putting. Finally, he reached up and took off his sunglasses, and she saw that he was missing an eye.

"Just like that, huh?" he asked.

"There's no other way around it."

Apex smiled. "Well then, we'll just have to do as you ask. Problem is, those fighters out there? They're mine. They'll kill you as fast as they'd kill their own fathers if I told them to. Isn't that right, assassin?"

Robin took off her facemask, eyes full of hatred. "I was never one to believe in brainwashing and all that. Sorry."

A hint of annoyance flashed across Apex's face, and then he motioned to the group of pirates that surrounded him.

"Any of you here wanna be rich?" he asked. When they nodded, he smiled to reveal his blackened teeth. "Wonderful. Teach this bitch a lesson."

Two pirates rose first, and Valerie laughed. "Last chance. You're sure you want to do this?"

Apex just continued to smile.

"All right," Valerie said. "But do try to keep your blood off my dress."

"I thought we were playing it cool?" Robin said, drawing her sword. Martha and River had already stepped away, blending in with the crowd.

"We have a world waiting on us," Valerie said, drawing both swords as the pirates advanced. "We don't have time to play it cool."

Swords clashed. Soon the room was up in arms, but Valerie pushed the nearest attacker back with a kick and then sliced into the next.

"Go!" she shouted to Robin. "Check the slaves, see if your parents are among them."

"But you—"

"I can handle myself," Valerie said, and continued dodging attacks, slicing through opponents, and simply dealing with these assholes.

Robin put her mask back on as she darted past attacking pirates, hacking her way to the doors. She caught sight of Martha and River slipping out under a tent flap, and made her way over to them after exiting.

"Get back to the ship, bring it around and fire on the tent with all you've got."

"But… Valerie?" Martha asked.

"Trust me, she'll be just fine."

The two ran off, and Robin turned to the groups of slaves. They had all stopped fighting and were turned, looking toward the tent, most with confusion, some with determination. Before they had their chance to join the fight without knowing what it was about, she had to act.

She ran over to the point directly between them and the tent, lifted her swords, and dropped them.

"We are not here to fight you!" she shouted. "We're here to give you your freedom."

A woman stepped forward. "You'll get us all killed, along with yourselves!"

"Who are you to stand there and tells us how it is?" another demanded.

"I was like all of you," she replied. "But… worse. There's a reason I can't take this mask off, not in the sunlight, anyway."

A gasp rose out from a few of the fighters, and one said, "So, it's true? Your kind do exist?"

She nodded.

"We have no reason to believe her!" the first woman shouted.

"You do!" Robin replied, stepping toward them. "My mother and father, they are among you!"

There was a pause of silence, and then a new one stepped forward, one no older than sixteen, she guessed.

"Not among us," he said. "Not if they were old enough to be your parents."

"What do you mean?"

"The old… some were too sickly, and they…"

"They were killed," the loud woman finished for him. "The rest are in Toro as the pirate counsel's personal slaves, or servants, if you want to play pretend."

Robin took that one hard, stepping back with the shock of it. She had thought this could be it. So close, yet so far away.

"And when I go after them?" she asked. "What awaits me?"

The boy shook his head, eyebrows raised. "You want to go in there? We're not talking some outpost. We're talking a city of old, entirely populated by no-good cut-throats, murderers with no loyalty but to themselves. More than likely, your parents would be serving one of the pirates in the city center, or the fortress, as they call it now. None of this running in guns blazing shit, or they'll be dead along with every other slave in the city. So, are you ready to commit to that?"

She shrugged. "Sounds like another day in my life, lately."

"Then I'm in," he said, and started walking forward. Several others broke ranks, too, and joined him, walking towards her.

"You're all going to get us killed!" the woman shouted. "Get back here!"

"We've been looking for a way to escape this," the man said. "Whether this is it or not, I intend to find out."

The others muttered in agreement, and just then a pillar of the tent snapped behind them, followed by the form of Valerie as she backed out, surrounded by ten pirates. In a flash, she had charged them, sword cutting through and sending blood to wet the parched earth.

They all fell back like wilting flowers.

"That one's with us," Robin said, and then motioned them forward. "Join us, fight for your freedom."

She led the charge, and her group of new recruits followed close behind. A glance over her shoulder showed that only the one loud woman and a few stragglers remained behind. A second later, they were running for the hills.

Another wall of the tent fell down, this time to a new wave of bullets, and it was followed by Apex. He was smiling, in spite of the death and destruction being rained down on his people, and he simply pointed up.

Valerie and Robin both looked up at the same time, horrified to see the sun blocked out by two of the smaller blimps they had followed here.

As the blimps above started unloading shots on the ground around them, fighters on both sides started falling to the shots as Valerie and Robin dove out of the way, a tall, thin man stepped out to join Apex. Judging by the extravagant gold trim on his red hat and his long coat, this could only be the Prince.

"You just couldn't handle her?" the Prince said to Apex in disgust.

He held two rail guns over his shoulders, larger than any Robin had seen before, and tossed one to Apex.

Robin ran for them, narrowly dodging the first rail gun blast that came her way. It hit the tent behind her, which burst into flames. Two pirates came at her from the left, cutlasses flailing, and she had to stop, dodge under the first attack and then step back to avoid the second, and that's when the next rail blast hit her.

It was like a pillar of fire right through her side, and everything in her wanted to simply shrivel up and die.

She screamed out in pain as one of the cutlasses took her in the shoulder.

"FUCK!" That hurt, too, but this time she was too pissed to be distracted by the hit. Barely able to stand from the pain, she lunged for the closest guy, the one whose blade was still lodged inside her.

Teeth sunk into flesh and she spun, drinking his blood, eyes flaring red. The other backed up, then took off running with piss running down his leg. Another rail blast came, but she let the pirate in her arms absorb the blast. Blood trickled down her neck like the delicate fingers of a lover, and for a moment, she imagined Valerie there with her, consuming this man's life.

And then she pulled her teeth away, licking her lips with a satiated, ecstatic disgust. This wasn't her, or it hadn't been. But now?

JUSTIN SLOAN & MICHAEL ANDERLE

She let him fall to the ground, feeling her energy and will to fight return, and yanked the cutlass from her shoulder.

These guys wanted to play like that? Fine.

There was still a hole in her side, but she felt the blood working its magic, and was sure it wouldn't be a problem for too long. Right now, she had pirates to kill.

At the tent, pirates were streaming forth, shouting about the flames and leaping into the fight. Smoke concealed some of the view, the chaos of it all adding to their fog of war.

Another rail gun blast hissed past her ear, hitting a pirate behind her that she hadn't seen. She hefted the cutlass and leaped.

Mid-air, she saw the rail gun firing up to shoot, but she smiled. She knew she was faster. The blade knocked the gun aside and she was on the Prince in a second, except that, just as her teeth were sinking into him, Apex came at her with a large metal object that fit around his hand and provided a battering ram style strike when it hit her.

She went flying off of the Prince, rolling across the ground and coughing up dirt that had flown into her mouth.

This close to finding her parents, she wasn't going down so easy.

A rail gun blasted the ground beside her, and she rolled aside again, then was up, claws out, ready for the three pirates who had emerged from the partially collapsed tent. She took out the first two with a claw to the gut and another to the neck, then picked up the third by the neck and balls, and charged the Prince.

Blast after blast took out the pirate so that, by the time she reached the Prince, there was only the head and pelvis. She tossed them at him and they made a nice thud that splattered blood on the two pirate leaders, and then smiled at the sight of Valerie. The older vampire had just taken down what looked like twenty pirates, and was moving in on Apex.

He spun and tried to use that battering-ram puncher, but she was too fast, dodging out of the way so that he was off balance.

When he spun back again, she was waiting, swords in hand, and skewered him with both swords, like a crisscross kebab, before pulling the swords out and across so that he split apart like he'd been cut open with very evil scissors.

"Argghh!" the Prince screamed and hit the rail gun across his leg so that it started sending sparks into the air. When he lifted it to fire again, the shots were fast, but erratic. More of the tent burst into flames, along with other buildings. He spun, not caring who or what he hit along the way, just trying to get a shot in on either of them.

Meanwhile, Martha's blimp above finally scored a devastating blow against one of the enemy blimps, which exploded before starting to fall.

Seeing this, the Prince appeared even more enraged. He hefted up the second rail gun and, with incredible effort, sent shots with both, first at Valerie and then Robin. Forced to dive for cover, since she was still feeling the pain from the last time one of those shots connected, she glanced around for a way out of this that didn't involve getting shot.

Not far off was a dead pirate with throwing knives. She had become quite skilled with knives, so turned to make a dash for it when the sun hit some exposed skin where she had been shot. A new wave of pain went over her, and she trembled, turning around and holding the spot, trying to cover it. The skin had already started growing back, but that also left her vulnerable to the sun.

Valerie must've seen this, because she shouted, "Hang tight!" and a second later, the Prince went flying through the air, screaming.

He landed with a thud, and now it was Robin's turn. She kept her exposed side to the ground, pulling the fabric of her torn clothes as tight as she could, which wasn't much because of the

Kevlar layer over most of it. Reaching the dead pirate, she tore his coat from him, quickly tied it around herself so that she was covered, and then spun back to see the Prince had recovered and was aiming in at Valerie. She saw him, too, and was ready to act, but Robin made the first move. The first knife left her fingers as if it were a part of her, simply moving away temporarily. It flew with speed and accuracy, connecting with him square in the hand that held the gun. When it fell, it sent a blast out that nearly hit Valerie, and she shouted, "Watch it!"

"Sorry, but watch this one," Robin said, flicking out another knife so that it connected with the Prince's eye.

He shouted in pain, screaming, reaching for a pistol tucked into the back of his exuberant coat. But, before he could reach it, Valerie said, "Oh, you like that? How about a bit of teamwork."

She darted forward, almost quicker than Robin could even see, and landed with a flying kick that connected with the hilt of the knife. The knife went clean through the Prince's head and came out the other side, and then he collapsed.

Just then, the second enemy blimp burst into flame, and cheering arose from the line of slaves who had joined Robin's side. She turned, beaming, totally ignoring the itch of pain that remained from where she'd been hit with the blaster and then by the cutlass.

They had done it. Not only that, they had their own little army to invade Toro with.

They all stood, watching the place burn to the ground, and she felt this was a new beginning. One forged from flame, and one that could only end in chaos.

She was looking forward to the fight of taking Toro down, now that she'd tasted the thrill of it. Or maybe her excitement just had to do with the fresh blood she had consumed. Either way, she smiled at Valerie and stepped into the shadow before beckoning her over. Valerie approached, and when the woman met her just at the edge of the shadows, she pulled back her mask, took her in her arms, and pulled her in until their lips were pressed firmly together.

When Valerie pulled back in shock, they stared at each other for a moment, and then Robin pulled her in. This time they didn't hold back... well, on the kissing anyway. There were way too many men and women watching and cheering for it to be more than that.

EPILOGUE

Slaver's Peak

By the time the blimp had landed and the fires had burned to ash, Valerie and Robin had settled everyone down and briefed them on the plan.

"Go if you have a home to return to," Valerie had said, "or join us in taking down the bastards who tried to take away your freedom."

All had stayed, all ready to exact their revenge. To have their justice.

Valerie hailed Martha, and the groups made their way to the blimps. There was this ship, the others that the Prince had taken over, and several more. Certainly enough to invade Toro.

"Let's get to it then," Valerie said, and everyone boarded.

When Martha had them in the air, ready to follow one of the fighters who claimed he knew the way, she smiled to Valerie and Robin.

"Why don't you two go get some rest, I know you need it."

Valerie smiled. "I'll be fine."

Martha chuckled, and said, "Are you sure?"

"Yeah," Robin added, the corner of her mouth going up. "Are you sure?"

Valerie blushed, then nodded to Martha and followed Robin to the stairs that led below deck. Here she took her by the wrist.

"Are you sure?" she asked. "I mean, about all this? About that kiss."

Robin bit her lip, hand taking Valerie's side and pulling her close. "We don't know what's about to happen, but I know this— I'm either about to be reunited with my parents, or I'll be dead. Either way, I think some well earned rest with you is the perfect way to spend however long it takes for us to get there."

Valerie let out the breath she'd been holding, hoping Robin would say something like this, then allowed the younger woman to lead her by the wrist down and into the small room toward the back of the ship.

It was dark, but that didn't stop Valerie from being able to see as the younger vampire slipped out of her clothes and then turned, fully exposed, and motioned her forward. Valerie's heart beat faster than any vampire's should have been able to, and then she slipped out of her pirate dress, took the woman in her arms, and felt her tongue brush gently across her own.

Damn, she wished this ride would take forever, but she knew it couldn't. In the meantime, she was damn sure going to make every second count.

All I can say right now is WOW. I just finished writing this book and my book 2 in the Age of Magic books (*Shades of Dark*), and ran off to finish reading PT Hylton's Age of Magic book, *Storm Raiders*. I love what we're doing in this universe, and reading the reviews I am super thrilled to see that you all do too.

I also read the *The Dark Night* and was excited to see that, not only is it an awesome story (my new favorite of the KGU?), but it had pirates! And... pirates are what made up a lot of *Born into Flames*, as you know. I was about half way through writing when I picked up Michael's book, and it was encouraging to see how he had approached it and how the audience was gobbling it up.

What I attempted to do here was show another part of this future / post apocalyptic world, one where a group of people looked for a way to survive and found it in reverting to the old ways -- piracy. As you saw in *Justice is Calling* and the pirates there, these pirates can range from deadly scary to pretty much ridiculous and silly. That's what I want to do in these books. I want some characters that you think 'DAMN!' about, and others that make you giggle (or chuckle or at least give it a half-smile).

I hope we've accomplished that here! As I write this, I'm at the stage where now Michael is going to run his magic fingers across the keyboard and add some sparks of amazingness, so what you all get will likely be even better than what I envisioned. But I'd love to hear from you, because book 6 is ALREADY underway, and you probably have some opinions on the matter. We'd love to hear them in either email or, especially if they are simply kind words, in the reviews for this book.

Going forward: The way we have it now, book 6 will be the end of this arc, and then another arc begins. I have lots of cool ways this all could go, and ideas for spinoff characters, if we ever wanted to go that route.

Craig Martelle and I are outlining a cool spinoff novel that takes some of our stories and puts them tighter and that will lead to some of the most amazing next arcs you've ever seen (okay, wishful thinking on my part. Or... hopeful thinking). Regardless, I'll have a blast doing it, and I know many of you and know that you'll be right there at our sides for the ride.

Until then, thank you as always - you all make this dream a reality! Without you reading the books I couldn't be doing this full-time, and without your emails and Facebook messages to tell me how much you love the books, I'd probably lose myself in the depths of reading negative reviews.

On the note of children - we just found out we're having our third! That was always our goal, so we're beyond excited. Of course, that means I have to write extra hard and fast before February, knowing I'll be out of commission for at least a few days when the baby comes. Luckily our other two kids are in daycare, or I would be in trouble!

More to come on that, and more books soon too! Like I mentioned above, *Shades of Dark* will be hitting the shelves shortly, if not by the time you finish reading this one. The Age of Magic is going in some great directions, and I think you'll love that series. Some people have felt the series in general is darker, or that it kind of destroys everything we've built here (by what it says happened to the world in the distant future), but I would argue that and say - keep reading and you'll see. Big plans ahead!

AUTHOR NOTES - MICHAEL ANDERLE

WRITTEN JULY 7TH, 2017

I will not weep, I will not weep...

First, THANK YOU for not only reading this book, but for reading all of the way to the END (and my Author Notes.)

Justin mentioned it before, but I'll reiterate. The Kurtherian Gambit fanbase has provided him an opportunity to try full time writing.

Until he didn't...then he did, again. More to come about *that* comment.

You see, *RIGHT* after Justin quit his previous full time job (and wrote the author notes for our last book with Valerie) his dream job came calling, with their hat in their hand.

Or rather, with the salary he wanted the first time they talked and he couldn't take the job.

For any creative, you have certain stories, or characters you might LOVE to work with and this company was offering that to Justin.

And like the little bastards (sorry, like the little tempters) they were, they enticed him to come work full time on their project.

Then, reality set in.

I understood Justin's desire to work on their property (I don't know if I'm at liberty to say who it was… but it might have been someone in the Marvel, DC, Star Wars, <insert additional large and cool places to write here> arena - just to give you an idea *WHY* it might have tempted the man.)

The problem was Justin had already tasted freedom…Sorry, he had already tasted the ability to write on his own work during the day and had lived the dream for a little while before the fall… Err, before the additional opportunity to experience working in a well known and (kinda) life long dream job.

He found out the grass wasn't greener…<Damn, I keep trying to keep this polite>

Justin found out that his heart was back at home, working full time on his own stories and now? Now he is #WritingLikeA-SonofaBitch and I am having to work to make sure his output is fed (covers, editors, JIT teams, audio).

Personally, it is a really cool feeling to me that just eight (8) short months after our first book came out, that we (you, me, TKG etc.) played some part in his professional life.

I guess since I was a kid, I've always wanted to be 'special' in some way. In my teen's, it was thinking I could be a rock star, up on stage.

<Hey! Don't judge me, I bet many of you might agree with my dreams - LOL>

Anyway, spandex aside, it didn't happen. Not only because I couldn't carry a tune if it came with a handle, but I didn't have a clue how to even TRY to do it when I was younger.

Naive was my middle name… As I think about it, Ignorant was a possible *second* middle name. *Michael Ignorantly-Naive Anderle*…That was me.

Sorry, I digressed off into Rock Star land a moment.

The core of wanting to be a rock star was the desire to feel important in some way. As I grew older, wiser, and found out what really makes me tick more understanding has occurred. I realize I love being a part of the success (not necessarily financial, although that is cool) of those around me.

Meaning, I enjoy knowing that Death Becomes Her has meaning beyond the story. That book, and the effort to write it culminated in affected a man's life *I did not know at the time.* When I wrote it, I didn't know anything about Indie Publishing, Indie Author's (other than those I read ALL THE DAMN TIME) and never expected to get to know so many of you, the fans.

Before I tear up here (I am writing this author note in a public place, so sitting here weeping isn't high on my social activities I care to accomplish today) let me say *thank you* one more time.

Because you care, and you read, and you share - Justin M. Sloan's life has been changed along with his wife, and children.

Readers helping readers and authors.

I think maybe this is what publishing should have always been about. So, to those Publishers who have fucked up authors for decades with your crap marketing, horrible advances, and God knows what else?

Here is our middle-finger waving in your direction.

To those Publishers who have helped authors live and thrive and grow their stories and share them with fans young and old, here and abroad?

Here is my heart felt appreciation even though the story of YOUR support to those authors may never have been told.

We, the readers and the fans of Kurtherian Gambit SALUTE you!

Michael *(tearing up like a man who can sometimes be emotional)* Anderle

BOOKS BY JUSTIN SLOAN

SCIENCE FICTION

RECLAIMING HONOR (Vampires and Werewolves - Kurtherian Gambit Universe)

Justice is Calling

Claimed by Honor

Judgment has Fallen

Angel of Reckoning

Born into Flames

Defending the Lost

Return of Victory

Shadow Corps (Space Opera Fantasy - Seppukarian Universe)

Shadow Corps

Shadow Worlds

Shadow Fleet

War Wolves (Space Opera Fantasy - Seppukarian Universe)

Bring the Thunder

Click Click Boom

Light Em Up

Syndicate Wars (Space Marines and Time Travel - Seppukarian Universe)

First Strike

The Resistance

Fault Line

False Dawn

Empire Rising

FANTASY

The Hidden Magic Chronicles (Epic Fantasy - Kurtherian Gambit Universe)

Shades of Light

Shades of Dark

Shades of Glory

Shades of Justice

FALLS OF REDEMPTION (Epic Fantasy Series)

Land of Gods

Retribution Calls

Tears of Devotion

MODERN NECROMANCY (Supernatural Thriller)

Death Marked

Death Bound

Death Crowned

CURSED NIGHT (Supernatural Thriller with Werewolves and Vampires)

Hounds of God

Hounds of Light

Hounds of Blood (2018)

CONNECT WITH THE AUTHORS

Justin Sloan Social

For a chance to see ALL of Justin's different Book Series Check out his website below!

Website: http://JustinSloanAuthor.com

Email List: http://JustinSloanAuthor.com/Newsletter

Facebook Here:
https://www.facebook.com/JustinSloanAuthor

Michael Anderle Social

Website:
http://kurtherianbooks.com/

Email List:
http://kurtherianbooks.com/email-list/

Facebook Here:
https://www.facebook.com/TheKurtherianGambitBooks/

Made in the USA
Las Vegas, NV
16 May 2022